THE OTHERWOODS

THE OTHERWOODS

JUSTINE PUCELLA WINANS

BLOOMSBURY
CHILDREN'S BOOKS
NEW YORK   LONDON   OXFORD   NEW DELHI   SYDNEY

BLOOMSBURY CHILDREN'S BOOKS
Bloomsbury Publishing Inc., part of Bloomsbury Publishing Plc
1385 Broadway, New York, NY 10018

BLOOMSBURY, BLOOMSBURY CHILDREN'S BOOKS, and the Diana logo
are trademarks of Bloomsbury Publishing Plc

First published in the United States of America in September 2023
by Bloomsbury Children's Books

Bloomsbury books may be purchased for business or promotional use.
For information on bulk purchases please contact Macmillan Corporate and
Premium Sales Department at specialmarkets@macmillan.com

Library of Congress Cataloging-in-Publication Data
available upon request
ISBN 978-1-5476-1254-3 (hardcover) • ISBN 978-1-5476-1255-0 (e-book)

Book design by Jeanette Levy
Typeset by Westchester Publishing Services
Printed and bound in the U.S.A.
2 4 6 8 10 9 7 5 3 1

To find out more about our authors and books
visit www.bloomsbury.com and sign up for our newsletters.

To all the queer kids reading this,
whether you are slaying monsters
or hiding under the covers,
you are heroes
and you are magic.

THE OTHERWOODS

1

The Monster
Under the Bed

River Rydell always knew they were destined for greatness, but they were very determined to make sure it didn't happen.

There must have been some mistake anyway. River read a lot of books and played a lot of video games, so they knew the makings of a hero. Heroes were boys or girls who had many skills and few fears, who weren't afraid to answer the call of adventure. River wasn't a boy or a girl, didn't have any skills outside reading and playing video games, had plenty of (perhaps even too many) fears, and always thought the call of adventure was better left ignored.

But for some almost funny and mostly rude reason, The Otherwoods chose River.

It started with the unfortunate circumstances of their

birth. Not unfortunate because their parents didn't want them, or because some aspect of the baby process didn't work right. Unfortunate because River was born with the cursed ability to see spirits.

The ability to see spirits? you might be thinking. *That sounds completely awesome! An opportunity to be something bigger, something more!*

No, nope, absolutely not, River would tell you.

The magic of seeing spirits wasn't something humans could actually use. It wasn't a superpower. Instead, it revealed all the inhuman, the no-longer human, the kinda-but-not-actually human—the spirits and the spirit*ish* and the monsters.

The monsters were the worst of them all.

Seeing spirits wasn't a gift. It was freaking terrifying.

And The Otherwoods was where magic lived—a world overlapping our own, where monsters reign. A world where the darkness of magic runs free, and humans don't belong. A world that kept inviting River in.

Even the human spirits that River saw shivered at the very thought of the place. They would cringe, walking by River and spotting the portals that opened whenever River was around.

"Don't go into The Otherwoods," they said.

"Poor dear, the monsters will eat you up," they said.

River pretended not to hear the spirits (acknowledging them would only make things worse), but the words stayed with them. It certainly wasn't a good feeling to have even the dead pity you.

The Otherwoods had started calling to River before they could remember, before they heard its name—the earliest invitation a literal open gate that doubled as a portal (a little on-the-nose, but understandable as River was maybe four at the time and not very smart). They took one look past the white painted planks and into the foggy air and blood-splattered trees with branches bent like broken bones and said NO, NOPE, ABSOLUTELY NOT (in their four-year-old, not-very-smart way) and turned in the other direction.

Now, River was twelve and a half and very smart, so The Otherwoods grew craftier.

River had learned the warning signs of a possible portal. A glimmer in the air, a sudden shift of temperature, that odd little feeling that the familiar is no longer familiar but something stomach-turning and strange.

Honestly, it was better to avoid wooded areas altogether. Any bump in the night, moving shadow, scare fodder of any sort—all of it should be completely and totally ignored. There was no way to tell if it was just imagination, or The Otherwoods calling. River did not want to take their chances. They didn't interact with spirits—human spirits, animal spirits, or spirits in between. Even if spirits weren't a trap or a portal, they were just as scary.

Not as scary as monsters, though. Because monsters could touch you, if they knew you were looking.

So while River had managed to avoid going into The Otherwoods all this time, they couldn't stop The Otherwoods from coming to them.

Most people can't tell when things creep out of the dark

Otherwoods and sneak into our world. A few hairs may rise on their arms or a slight sinking feeling may settle in their gut, but most people wouldn't experience anything more than that. Despite their best efforts, River was not most people.

River saw everything that slipped through, and wished they didn't. It was like the monsters from The Otherwoods knew exactly how to find them—like they had some connection to River. And the connection felt stronger with some monsters than with others.

Like Charles, the monster under River's bed.

River always took a long time to shut off the little lamp at the side of their bed, and tonight was no different. They knew Charles would be there, waiting for them in the darkness, just as he had been ever since he first crawled into River's bedroom a few months ago. Most of the monsters left when River didn't give them attention, and River had learned the hard way not to. It was back in their years as a small child, when they first saw a monster. It was a disgusting thing, some strange combination of a bird and a slug, with dripping, tar-like feathers, squishy skin, and a razor-sharp beak. River took one look in the creature's eyes and screamed.

It did not go well.

The monster tried to grab River's arm with slimy talons, and they were only saved when their mom came into the room and unknowingly stopped it by closing the window on its neck.

It had been an all-around terrible thing to experience, and River vowed from that day forward to never let the monsters know they could see them.

And it worked. Without attention, the monsters came and went. But not Charles. Instead of finding his way back to The Otherwoods, he took up lodging in the dark space between the mattress and the floor.

Currently, the lamp with its orange shade cast a warm and comforting glow over the room. It cut through the darkness, aside from some shadowy corners that River refused to look at anyway. They had thought naming Charles might make him less scary, but it just made him a more familiar kind of scary: like spiders, standardized-test days, or talking to cute girls.

Only much, much worse.

"Charles" might sound nice, but monsters of the under-the-bed variety were rarely nice, and even a pleasant name didn't stop them from becoming a thing of nightmares.

So River didn't want to shut off the light. But if they kept the light on, Mom or Dad would come to their room and ask what was wrong or tell River to put away their phone and go to bed. River didn't want to admit that something was still going on, because then their parents would worry and Charles would know that River could see him.

Not that Mom or Dad had believed River when they tried to explain what they saw. Neither had the school guidance counselor, or the therapist, or the psychologist.

No one believed River, so River had simply stopped talking about it.

Now, in bed, with the covers up to their belly, River kept their chin up and their face forward. They could do this. They had to do this. They needed to sleep, after all.

But that didn't mean they had to do it alone.

River crawled out of bed, trying not to wince when their first foot sank into the rug—in clear reach from where Charles spent his time. Keeping their footsteps light, they moved toward their bedroom door. River generally didn't like the nighttime, because everything was scarier in the dark. River had enough to be afraid about in daylight.

Also, creatures from The Otherwoods preferred the night, which made it so much worse.

River's adrenaline was pumping, so they started walking with T-Rex arms, making little stomps to the other side of the room. Nobody in the scary books and shows River read and watched had anything bad happen to them while walking like a dinosaur. River felt silly and a little babyish, but couldn't help but smile. No one could see them anyway.

Aside from maybe Charles, but it didn't matter if a monster thought River was strange.

River opened their bedroom door with a creak. They froze, making sure the sound hadn't woken up their parents, or something scarier. They breathed out a sigh of relief on seeing that the coast was clear. The only thing in sight was their partner in crime, Mr. Fluffy Pancakes.

Sure, the cat's name had become embarrassing, but after five years, River's mom insisted it was too late to change it. River was convinced she didn't want to let them ever live it down. Mostly, River referred to the cat as just Pancakes, because it was marginally better.

Not that it really mattered. Pancakes didn't care if he was just Pancakes or Mr. Fluffy Pancakes or That Stupid

Cat, as River's dad called him. Pancakes knew who he was whatever he was called, and River had to respect that. Besides, embarrassing names didn't matter around their parents, who were always embarrassing. And it wasn't like River invited anyone over anyway.

How could they, with a Charles no one else would be able to see?

Bending over, River scooped up all fifteen pounds of Pancakes, who immediately started purring, and rushed back into their bedroom.

No sign of Charles yet. River felt a little better, especially now with Pancakes by their side.

They got back into bed, Pancakes curling up in a ball at their feet. River kissed the top of Pancakes' head, stroked his gray fur once, and lay flat against their pillow.

Holding their breath, they shut off the light.

Almost immediately, a long, bladed arm reached out from under the bed. A buzzing rattle, like a metallic cicada, echoed through the bedroom. Charles dug the pincers at the end of his limb into the fabric of the bed to pull himself out from his hiding spot.

Pancakes hissed loudly, drawing the monster's attention.

River looked at the large form, sharp and bug-like, with huge pincers and a slimy exoskeleton. Little hairs sprouted from areas on Charles's limbs, which somehow made his appearance more disgusting. Charles was a nightmarish blend of praying mantis and earwig, glistening dark and making sounds like River's stomach if they ate too quickly.

He had to be a bug monster. Not that other types of

monsters were much better, but River was already afraid of normal bugs. Six-foot-tall versions were a whole new level of terrifying.

River was glad they had already gone to the bathroom.

Charles turned his bug eyes back toward River, pincers clamping as he gave some call that was a cross between a growl and a groan. He leaned toward River, ignoring the hisses of Pancakes, now twice his normal size in fur alone.

Charles lifted his gnarly limbs higher into the air, poised to strike, as some slimy liquid dripped off him.

Not today, Charles.

River pretended to see right through the monster, before turning to the other side and squeezing their watering eyes shut.

Eventually, the clicking and buzzing noises quieted as Charles returned to his habitat under River's bed. Pancakes kneaded the blanket and made himself comfortable enough to fall back asleep.

River wanted to scream, but kept their eyes closed and pulled the blanket up higher. They wished they were brave, that they lived up to their twelve years and stopped acting like a baby. But giant bug monsters were a problem that made bravery too high a hurdle.

They didn't like that about themself. They also didn't think it was anything they could change. It was who they were, in the same way Pancakes was a cat and Charles was a horrible otherworldly monster.

River Rydell had a unique ability, but they were certainly no hero.

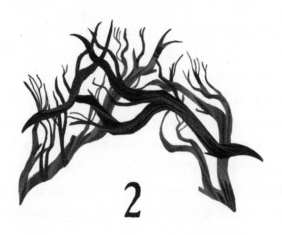

2

The Monster at School

If there was any time of day that River dreaded more than the nightly Charles encounter, it was Ms. Deery's fourth-period history class. She was the type of monster that everyone could see, but no one knew how to stand up to. It was practically a curse to be placed on the Wildcat team in sixth grade, where you had no choice but to have her as a teacher. River hadn't understood why some kids were crying back in August at their team placements, but now that River had spent nearly a full year with Ms. Deery, they would've gone back in time and started crying too.

River took a deep breath outside the classroom door, clutching their books so tightly their knuckles shone white. They stepped inside right as the bell rang.

"Late again, River," Ms. Deery said.

Except she didn't say "River." She said a different name that made River feel like they'd been hit with a brick. And made them wish that they could hit Ms. Deery with a brick too, but she was old and it would probably break her hip.

She looked particularly sinister in her ruffled white blouse and long skirt that didn't seem to come out of any recent century. Sometimes River wondered if she was a spirit that stuck around for the sole purpose of tormenting children.

River opened their mouth to correct Ms. Deery, but no words came to them. River was used to simply closing their eyes and ignoring her like they did all the other monsters, so they couldn't respond. And there certainly weren't any bricks around.

"*River* was in before the bell," Avery Davis said, rolling her eyes at Ms. Deery.

River's heart beat a little bit faster. Avery Davis was one of the most popular girls in the sixth grade, and for good reason. She was smart, pretty, friendly, and stood up against horrible teachers who deadnamed students without any apology.

From the very first day in fifth grade when River came out as nonbinary and reintroduced themself to their classmates, Avery had been on their side. She never got their pronouns wrong, and corrected others without making too big a deal about it. She even said hi to River every morning *and* the few times they ran into each other outside school.

There was nothing *not* to like about Avery—and River had tried.

As amazing as Avery Davis was, River couldn't let themself get close to people. River had watched enough scary movies to know that some people put curiosity before personal safety. That some people investigated bumps in the night and strange sounds outside their windows. What if Avery was the type to wander into portals to nightmare worlds?

River couldn't deal with those kinds of people!

Plus, if River and Avery did get close, that might cause The Otherwoods to take notice. It had tried before to trick River with the things they loved: a rare Pokémon trading card, a batch of chocolate chip cookies, an advance copy of the last book in River's favorite series—all conveniently placed just inside a sneaky portal. River would never put another person at risk of being used by The Otherwoods like that. It was bad enough their parents had to be involved, but for some reason, The Otherwoods never seemed to engage with them. (Maybe their mom had developed a reputation after snapping that monster's neck.)

Either way, it was better if River kept to themself. It was hard enough to pretend everything was okay when a monster or wayward spirit came into view while River was alone. If River did make a friend, it'd only be a matter of time before River scared them. Who wouldn't think something was wrong with them? Their parents did, and the counselor/therapist/psychologist/occasional nosy neighbor did too.

Not that everyone at school *didn't* think so already. River ignored the spirits and monsters as much as they could, but because they usually looked freaked out, they got a bit of their own reputation. Plus, there was that one time they started crying in the middle of math class because a portal appeared right outside the door and they refused to leave until it disappeared.

That one sent them back to the guidance counselor, and almost set them back three years of pretending to be okay to their parents.

Being nonbinary already made River stand out enough. Being nonbinary and supposedly unstable only made matters worse. The other kids weren't necessarily mean to River's face, but the kids avoided them, and River was no stranger to the occasional weird look.

Being alone was for the best, but sometimes, it didn't feel like it.

Which is why even the smallest things like smiles and hellos from Avery Davis made the world feel brighter and gave them some strange butterflies in their stomach—or maybe dragonflies, which were like butterflies but more intense and cooler.

River took a seat in the back, hoping Ms. Deery would leave them alone so she could drone on in her lecture and forget to move the mouse cursor out of the way when she played videos. If they could get through the rest of class without Ms. Deery looking at them again, it would be a pretty good day.

Considering.

The good thing about ignoring monsters all the time

was that it made it easier to ignore the stares from the other kids.

It didn't help to be deadnamed in front of the whole class. River knew they shouldn't be embarrassed because someone was being awful to them, but they really didn't like to be the center of attention in any way. And they certainly didn't like to show that they were too scared to say anything back.

My name is River, they scrawled on their notebook, *and if you don't call me by my name, I'll report you to the principal.*

You mean, crusty witch, River added, then immediately crossed it out.

Aside from reading and playing video games, River was also extremely skilled in thinking of things to say long after the fact. It was the second thing they most disliked about themself, the whole scary-monster-vision business being the first.

River tried to sink into their hoodie like it could swallow them up. It had yet to work, but stranger things had certainly happened.

When River first explained to their parents how they felt about their gender, they said they didn't want to be seen as a boy or a girl, just as River. But the truth was, River didn't want to be seen at all. It felt like every day, there was a new reason for them to stick out. And it wasn't only The Otherwoods they had to worry about. River's mom was right: middle school was tough.

And it got even worse when, out of the corner of their eye, River saw a shadow. They gulped down some air and almost coughed it back up. *Why now?*

Using their peripheral vision, River saw the full form of the monster. It was dark and blobbish, with long sharp teeth that looked like needles. It moved across the floor like a mechanical mop, and overall seemed like one of those deep-sea creatures that should never see the sun.

River's chest grew tight as they tried not to watch the monster's bulging eyes take in all the kids. It left slime on Mateo Ramos's desk, and brushed the hair of Lu Smith, but River couldn't do anything about that. It wasn't like anyone else could see the monster anyway.

Then, like every other monster and spirit, the monster took a big interest in River. It slid right up to River's desk, staring directly at them. River could feel some of its ooze hit their leg and tried desperately not to cringe. Instead, they pretended to furiously take notes, though they definitely weren't listening to whatever Ms. Deery was saying.

In fact, the notes they were taking weren't sensical at all, but a random assortment of words with the occasional *oh no so gross please help*

Luckily, monsters couldn't read human languages.

Unluckily, at that exact moment, the monster's bulging right eye decided to fall off its body. It hit the floor with a sickening plop before rolling right against River's shoe.

A burning burp caught in River's throat as they internally screamed what they externally could not. A tear or two may have leaked from River's eye, but, they hoped, maybe the rest of the class would chalk it up to Ms. Deery's earlier comment. The thought was embarrassing but better than the truth.

After what felt like forty years, the monster's eye rolled back to latch on to its oozing body, but didn't stop looking at River. A chill ran down their spine. They tried to turn into themself and focus on the paper in front of them, but a second face appeared on their right side. River jumped in their desk, swallowing a scream.

Ms. Deery snapped at them. "Rydell. Do you need a detention?"

Oh no. They didn't want to make a scene.

With wide eyes on their teacher, River watched as the face moved closer. It seemed to be attached to a wispy body, but River refused to actually look. From what they could tell, it was a humanlike spirit, although it had no lips and bright yellow eyes that dripped blood.

River wanted to scream, or throw up, or scream while throwing up if they could manage it.

"No," they weakly mumbled in response to Ms. Deery's glare.

They just wanted everyone to stop looking at them. They were stuck between a monster and a spirit, and the eyes on them made everything hotter.

The spirit giggled. Its voice was hoarse and crackly. "The Otherwoods is coming for you, child." River could feel its hot breath against their cheek. "And there will be no hiding this time."

River's stomach lurched, and in their shock, they made a mistake. For a split second, their eyes darted over to the spirit.

The spirit's sickening grin widened as blood dripped

into the hole of its mouth. "Can't ignore us forever, can you? Lucky I'm not a monster." Its yellow eyes shined as it leaned in. "But The Otherwoods will get you." It let out a screeching laugh that sprayed blood all over River's desk.

"River, are you okay?" Avery's loud whisper cut through the spirit's cackling.

"Um . . ." River's palms dotted with sweat and their vision clouded with white. The Otherwoods had tried to lure them in for years, but they somehow never considered *why*. They certainly wouldn't have dared ask anyway. If the spirit was telling the truth, it seemed like the answer would be clear to River soon enough.

And they knew it would be nothing good.

The room spun around them, and with the entire class still looking in their direction, the world went black.

3

The Potential Friend

River spent the rest of the day in the nurse's office, since neither of their parents could pick them up until school was out and River promised the nurse they were okay. They had to sip on a juice box and lie down, but were hardly able to rest with the threat the spirit had given them.

Normally, spirits didn't talk to them at all. They would make comments about them, and a few young spirits tried to pull on River's clothes or make silly faces to get their attention, but there was never anything that filled them with this much dread.

River couldn't stop feeling nauseated every time they thought about it. Maybe it was just paranoia, but they could swear they saw more shadows lurking in the nurse's office and the hallways. And when they stepped outside the building, clutching their backpack tightly, there were a handful of forlorn spirits—human aside from one with two mouths and no nose—watching them with their unsightly frowns.

What was happening?

This didn't feel like the normal number of spirits. It was different, like they were preparing for something, or warning River about it. River's heart pounded at the thought. They wanted to get home.

River's dad was usually late to pick them up from school, though. It wasn't his fault; it just took some time to get there from work. River normally didn't mind. But normally, there wasn't strange behavior coming from every direction.

At the usual pick-up area, River immediately caught sight of discolored dirt in the planter to the right of the door, with a bent branch sticking out from it.

A definite portal to The Otherwoods. River could recognize that type of tree anywhere, and it certainly didn't belong with the half-grown flowers.

The spirits were one thing, but a portal already? River was pretty sure they saw one just two days ago. They stopped for a moment, unzipped their backpack, and pulled out their planner. River was supposed to use it for homework, but instead took notes on when the portals appeared. Sometimes things were less scary when you knew to expect them.

They flipped through pages. For months, they had seen a portal maybe every two weeks, sometimes once a week. But another after only two days? That had never happened.

River's hand trembled as they marked an *X* in the little box that represented the date and jotted down the time. They quickly shoved everything away and zipped up their backpack, not wanting to be close to this new portal for much longer.

Trying their very best to breathe normally, River texted their dad to meet them by the Starbucks down the street. It was only a block or two over, and a bunch of people went there after school. River supposed a portal could pop up in the middle of a Starbucks as well, but on the off chance The Otherwoods had it in for twelve-year-olds in particular, the kid-to-adult ratio would probably be better.

River wished someone could help them figure out what the threat meant, and why there were more portals than usual. They knew it was better not to get anyone else involved (not that anyone would believe them anyway), but sometimes the fear morphed into loneliness. These weren't the kind of things someone should worry about at all, especially not alone. But they would have to figure it out themself somehow, even though they weren't good at that either.

There was still a slight chill in the air, but it felt more like spring clinging on than another Otherwoodsy appearance. The sun was high with the promise of summer, and despite everything, River was excited about the prospect. They could stay in the safety of their own home, playing their Switch and catching up on shows and books. Sure, Charles was at home, and other terrifying monsters could wander in here and there, but there was some comfort in knowing that none of them had killed River yet—hadn't even really tried. The important thing was to stay out of The Otherwoods, and River had learned all the tricks. They made sure to avoid wooded areas (The Otherwoods loved the cover of trees), be cautious around any openings with portal potential (doors, windows . . . walk through without checking and boom—Otherwoods), and above all, ignore (or run far away from) anything remotely scary.

Of course, they hadn't expected all the rules they'd learned about the timing of portals to suddenly change.

It made them feel helpless and alone. Not only could they not escape the portals and the monsters, they couldn't even tell anyone about it. Just having someone to talk to might have made them feel a little better, but they didn't have that either.

Because while their parents loved them, they didn't believe them. And because of that, it felt like River didn't have anyone.

Still ready for any sight that didn't seem quite right, River held on to their backpack straps and walked away from the school and onto the sidewalk. They'd barely got a few steps down the main street when something unexplainably strange and completely unheard of happened.

"River! Wait up!"

It didn't sound like a spirit, and River knew that a monster couldn't be calling out to them. Even if a monster *was* calling out to them, it certainly wouldn't sound like their crush; it'd be more of a growl or hideous screech. Despite knowing that, they were still surprised to turn around and see Avery Davis, all smiles and shining brown eyes.

"Are you walking to Starbucks?" Avery asked.

River nodded, then said, "Only to meet my dad." They cringed a little. Meeting their dad at Starbucks was not cool, especially not when everyone else had friends. River didn't want Avery to think that their only friends were their *parents*. Sure, they didn't have friends, really, but cute girls didn't need to know that.

Maybe Charles could count? They spent a lot of time together.

River's chest tightened with fear at having to see him again later.

No, Charles definitely didn't count.

"Awesome," Avery said. "Can I walk with you?"

River had no idea why Avery would want to walk with them, but they'd be lying if they said they weren't happy she did. River glanced around quickly, but there were no signs of monsters or spirits or any Otherwoodsy business.

"Sure," River said. "Um, yeah, sure."

A master of communication.

River wondered if they should practice talking more on Pancakes, and then immediately wished they hadn't had a thought as sad as that one.

"Are you okay?" Avery asked. "Like, after what happened in class—"

"I'm good, fine, thanks," River interrupted. Although they felt anything but good and fine as they kept spotting the occasional spirit, still watching them. River tried to

21

calm their breathing and focus on the ground in front of them. "I just . . . didn't get enough sleep."

Not a total lie. River hadn't slept well since Charles had moved in.

Avery seemed to believe them enough. As the two started walking, she bit her bottom lip. "Sorry about Ms. Deery. She's the worst."

"It's okay," River said. They tightened their grip on their backpack. "Thanks, though. For correcting her."

"Of course, that's the least I can do!" Avery practically skipped when she walked. "Honestly, we should report her to the principal, or the superintendent. There has to be someone who can fire her already."

"It's fine," River said quickly. "We only have a few months left with her anyway."

As much as River loved the idea of Ms. Deery getting fired, or at the very least, of not having to be in the same building as her for seventh *and* eighth grade, River didn't want to be the reason for it. That would be more attention they didn't need.

And River was good at ignoring things anyway.

They stepped over a shadowy snake on the ground, trying not to be too obvious about it. Avery stomped right on its friend's head, but her foot went through it. Neither the snake-adjacent creature nor Avery had any idea of each other.

River thought it was kind of creepy that most people had interactions with monsters and spirits daily and didn't know, but River also thought that they themself would much prefer to be one of those people.

Knowing was even creepier.

"I was gonna ask you something . . . kind of personal," Avery said.

River froze. Had they looked weird when they stepped over the snake thing?

"Uh . . . sure," River said. It was practically their catchphrase at this point.

"How was it to tell your parents you were nonbinary?" Avery's eyes were big, her voice low. She quickly stood up straight. "Not trying to pry . . . but I think I'm . . . um, what's the word I found?" She pulled out her phone and opened the notes app. "Pansexual. It means you're attracted to someone regardless of their gender."

For a moment, River entirely forgot about the threat and the unusual abundance of monsters. They didn't want to say this was becoming one of the best days of their life— River wasn't a hopeful person. Perhaps the bar was low, perhaps they were just happy about the possibility of having their crush *not* being unrequited. Or at least, of having a friend who would understand.

People didn't usually talk to River, but Avery was here. Confiding in them! Like they were a trustworthy and capable person and not someone hiding from things no one else could see.

They couldn't mess this up.

"Oh," River said. "Thanks for sharing that with me.

Telling my parents was okay. They had a lot of questions, and they still do, but they try even when they don't completely understand, and that means a lot. But telling anyone can be scary."

Had that sounded all right? It was probably the most River had ever said to another classmate. That had to be a good thing.

They hoped.

"You're really brave for doing it, then," Avery said.

River almost laughed at that. "Brave" was not a word they'd use to describe themself. "I guess," River said, not wanting to be rude. "Just make sure you're ready to tell them; don't force yourself, you know? Like, if you don't, that's okay too."

River didn't really trust themself to give advice. They hadn't done it before. But that sounded nice enough. Avery's expression seemed thoughtful, but still pleasant. River didn't think they'd said the wrong thing yet.

"I want to . . ." Avery kicked a rock on the sidewalk in front of them. It skittered across the surface and dropped into the street. "Once I think of how to say it."

"That can be the hard part," River agreed.

It had taken River a while to find the words that explained exactly how they always felt. Even then, it didn't feel perfect. River wasn't sure there was a perfect way to say anything, and if there was, they certainly weren't the person to find it.

"Can I have your number?" Avery asked. She smiled. "To text you for support."

River nearly tripped over their own feet.

Sure, they didn't want to get too close to people. But this was different. This was someone who needed them. The same way they needed Pancakes when facing Charles. Being with someone else didn't make scary things *not* scary, but it made it feel bearable. Avery needed a Pancakes. And it felt good to be needed.

Besides, it was *Avery Davis.*

Avery handed her phone to River, and kept her hand held out for theirs. River stared for a moment before giving her their phone to exchange numbers.

They switched their phones back.

"Thanks, River. For real."

River felt their heart flutter in their chest, and they crossed their arms tightly to try to stop it. Avery was one of those people who it felt good to be around. So nice in a genuine way, like she really cared.

Avery was the opposite of the monsters and The Otherwoods. She was sunshine. The light loved her, shimmering in her eyes and kissing her golden-brown skin.

River felt safer in the shadows, unnoticed, but at the same time, they wanted to get to know her better.

They'd reached the Starbucks by this point, and River saw their dad's blue car already parked on the street. Through the windshield, he looked between River and Avery and gave a big smile and two thumbs-up.

It was so bad, it almost made River want to enter The Otherwoods to escape.

"That's my dad," River said. "I should get going."

"Want to hang out at my house tomorrow?" Avery asked quickly.

River didn't know what to say, but they found themself nodding.

"Great! I'll text you later!" Avery gave a wave before walking toward the coffee shop.

As she moved away, River saw a bit of a shadow, sliding over her skin. Something like the snake from earlier. But monsters couldn't touch people without locking eyes. Could they?

No. Just a trick of the light, they said to themself. *Everything's fine. She doesn't feel it, so they aren't* really *touching her.*

River turned and walked toward the car, but the bad feeling didn't loosen. After all, River knew better than to trust reasonable explanations.

4

The Disbelieving Family

It was very important to River's parents that they all ate dinner together every night. Mom and Dad were intense about it too, making sure that Pancakes was fed at the same time. It was a good thing River's mom couldn't see Charles, or she'd probably have set a place for him at the table as well.

Since the only empty chair was across from River, that wouldn't have made dinner with their parents any more comfortable.

They shifted on the seat, keeping their phone face up on their lap. That way, it was still visible to them without being obvious to their parents. Although River normally didn't check their phone during dinner, Avery Davis didn't normally have their number. After they exchanged numbers,

River had texted a quick hey, it's River to make sure she had their number too. Since then, River had been checking the screen every two minutes for a new notification.

No such luck. Had she been serious about River hanging out at her house? Or were they stuck to forever being school-only friends and not after-school friends?

Was it okay for River to refer to her as a friend?

They were trapped on that thought and the confusing nature of it all when their mom approached the table with a bowl of salad in one hand and a plate of tilapia in the other. She had been trying to make healthier dinners to help with River's dad's blood pressure. River wasn't allowed to complain, even though *their* blood pressure was just fine, and a pizza night once in a while probably wouldn't hurt anyone.

"How was school, River?" Mom asked as she sat down.

They took a sip of water, trying to think what the best answer would be. They didn't want their parents to worry about them too much, so they never brought up their severe lack of friends. They especially didn't want to bring up Ms. Deery. Their parents would make a big deal out of it and embarrass River more, and that would only give her better reason to hate River. But mentioning Avery was also dangerous.

Their parents must've felt so bad about all the unsuccessful therapy and the trouble River had in the past that they overcompensated by being way too enthusiastic and, therefore, embarrassing. River would have to be careful about how, exactly, they asked for permission to go to Avery's house.

For now, they'd just handle the school question. "Fine." It was really the safest answer.

River's dad clucked his tongue. "Only fine? No fun stories? New adventures? New *friends*?"

River's cheeks flamed. They knew Dad had seen them with Avery at Starbucks, but thought that the lack of questions about her on the ride home meant they were safe. Apparently not.

"It's school," River said, deflecting. "It's not supposed to be fun."

And an adventure was the last thing River wanted, especially with the threat from The Otherwoods looming. They took a bite of the fish their mom plopped onto their plate, but it wasn't exactly satisfying.

"That doesn't mean it *can't* be," their mom said. She gave a small smile that was a little strained, but still warm. "You know you can tell us anything, River. Right?"

River knew their mom thought that was true, and they appreciated it. But they also knew it wasn't true at all. More than anything, River wanted to spill everything about The Otherwoods and the portals coming more often and the fear that it would succeed in taking them. The fear that they'd be lost in that strange, scary place and never have a disappointingly healthy but wonderfully normal family dinner again.

They wanted to hug their parents as the three of them talked through all River's worries. They wanted to cry as their mom stroked their hair and their dad promised to make it all better. They wanted their parents to say everything would be okay, because they couldn't help but feel that it wouldn't.

But River knew that wouldn't happen, and so they didn't say any of that. "I know," they lied instead.

Pancakes jumped up onto the empty chair and slowly reached his paw toward the plate of fish. His eyes were wide and hungry. River scooted the plate closer to him. Right as Pancakes tried to steal a piece he'd gotten a claw into, River's mom intercepted him.

"Mr. Fluffy Pancakes has his own food." She pointed to the half-eaten food in his bowl, which ironically had stacks of waffles printed all over it.

River gave the cat a glance that they hope said, *I tried.*

Pancakes slowly blinked before glaring at River's mom and reluctantly returning to his food bowl.

"Your mom's right, though," River's dad continued between bites. "You don't have to keep things to yourself. We're here for you."

River sighed. "I'm fine, Dad. Really."

It wasn't like River never *tried* to tell them the truth. At least, when they were too young to know better. In the past, River would casually point out people who weren't there and ask about them. They would complain about monsters and talk about the scary-tree place. At first, River's parents thought they simply had an overactive imagination and joked to friends that River should be a writer someday.

But when River turned eight and the ghosts didn't leave, their parents decided that "an overactive imagination" was actually "something terribly wrong with River."

They didn't exactly say it that way, but River later figured it out.

They went through three therapists, two school counselors, a child psychologist (or was it a psychiatrist?), and River's aunt Melody, who acted like a psychic but really just owned a large number of crystals. All of them were certain that River *wasn't* seeing these things, and if they *were*, they certainly didn't exist. River might have *thought* they knew what was going on with themself, but they were just confused.

Sometimes it felt like the seeing-spirits conversation and the being-nonbinary conversation used the same awful script. Adults, even with the best intentions, were very good at telling River how wrong they were about themself. And River figured they would continue to do so no matter what. River could be murdered by monsters and everyone would tell their body they were simply imagining it.

Despite everything these professionals tried, things didn't change for River.

So they learned to lie about it instead.

River's phone buzzed loudly in their lap, bringing them back into the moment but unfortunately also drawing the attention of their parents. Especially because, without thinking, River smiled at Avery's name popping up on the screen. Their parents grinned widely like lions about to capture their prey.

"What's that smile?" River's mom asked. "Who's that?"

"Someone cute?" their dad added, drawing out the last syllable.

River's face heated up in a way that said *yes*. "No!"

Their mom practically squealed. "What's their name?

Would they like to come over for dinner? We'd love to meet them."

River couldn't look at her, so they focused on the fish instead. "No, Mom, it's no one." They realized they still needed to ask about the next day. "Well, it's a friend. She asked if I could come over tomorrow."

"I knew it! You don't smile like that at no one. Of course you can go." Their dad pretended to wipe away a tear. "Just yesterday, you were in diapers, and now you're going to be dating and kissing—"

River put their hands over their face. "Stop, Dad, please."

Secretly, their chest felt like it had filled with bubbles at the thought of dating and *kissing* Avery, but they didn't want their dad talking about it. It would be something they could imagine in detail later when trying to fall asleep.

"I can drive you there," River's mom said. "Just let me know the time."

"But we need to talk about our door-open rule," their dad added, pointedly. "You're like twenty years too young to—"

River stood up from the table, chair screeching as it moved back across the floor. "Okay, thanks, I have to go to the bathroom!"

They ran away from the table and into the bathroom like they were running from a monster. A monster might be preferable to that situation. At least a monster didn't tease them about *kissing*.

River's face flamed at the thought.

Trying to remove it all from their mind, they opened the texts from Avery.

I was about to come out to my parents!
But I chickened out lol

She also sent a GIF of a chicken dancing. River had to laugh, but they started typing a response.

Don't worry about it, just tell them when ur ready

Her response was almost immediate, and River could imagine her smile from the tone of the text.

Totally! And I have you now! Can you still come tomorrow? Mom said it's fine!

Yeah, my parents said I can!

Yayayayayayay

River was about to send a smiley face, when another text from Avery came through.

Still, I wish I was as brave as you

Their immediate response would have been what are you talking about have you seen me? But they deleted that before they could finish all the letters. River bit their lip as they typed back, I'm not actually that brave, or brave at all, but deleted that too. What they actually sent was I'm here whenever :)

It made River happy to know that they were there for

someone. Even if Avery couldn't be there for them. At least, not in the way they really needed. She'd never believe River.

Would she?

They didn't get the chance to think about it much, because Avery responded with GIFs of dancing cats and raccoons and then asked what kind of shows and games River liked.

> I've been playing the new
> Pokemon game a lot

OMG I LOVE POKEMON

They kept texting back and forth, about things that couldn't be further from The Otherwoods' threats and monsters that weren't part of video games. They talked about school and what they'd do the next day together, and it was almost like spirits didn't exist. River stayed in the bathroom, sitting on the edge of the white tub and smiling at their phone, not paying any attention to the sun setting or the shadows creeping under the door.

5

The Issue with Closets

River never wanted to go into The Otherwoods, but they had given some thought to what they would bring if they were forced in. All the essentials that books promised would help with survival: the Swiss Army knife their dad had left on the kitchen counter that they snatched up (just in case), some rope, a flashlight, a lighter and backup matches, extra batteries, their cellphone charger (Did The Otherwoods have electricity? Perhaps a portable charger for some extra hours?), and a water bottle.

River had no idea, however, how to prepare for going to Avery's house.

Were they supposed to bring anything? A lighter and

rope wouldn't make the best impression with Avery, and especially not with her parents.

Maybe snacks?

River wasn't sure what to *wear*. It was a Saturday, so they had the time to figure something out. They stood in an old T-shirt from elementary school and underwear that they wore to bed, looking through their dresser.

Maybe they should check the closet.

River walked over to the closet door and twisted the handle. The blood rushed from their face as their normal array of patterned button-up shirts and sweatshirts was replaced with a thick layer of fog and shadowy trees that buzzed with energy. Something that sounded like a crow mixed with a dog caw-barked, and River yelped.

No, nope, absolutely not.

They shut the door on the portal immediately with a slam and pushed a chair in front of it.

The sinking feeling returned to their stomach. That was another portal with barely a day passing.

What was The Otherwoods up to?

River didn't know if they should be pleased or afraid that The Otherwoods had returned to their obvious portals. They were the type of person to err on the side of afraid.

"River? Are you all right?"

Their mom already had their bedroom door open and had fully stepped inside. It was an annoying habit that River had to deal with. Their mom had said she'd start knocking when River started helping with the mortgage.

River tried to give her twenty dollars from their birthday money stash, but River's mom simply laughed and said that wouldn't quite cut it.

How much could a mortgage be anyway?

More than the price of River's privacy, apparently.

"I'm fine." River answered quickly and out of breath, a sure sign that they were in fact not fine.

"Uh-huh . . . ," their mom said, eyeing the room. Aside from the messy, half-opened dresser drawers and the frightened, half-dressed River, there was nothing out of place, except . . . Her gaze landed on the chair wedged into the closet door handle. "What's in your closet?"

Oh, just a portal into a terrifying world of monsters, River could've said.

"Nothing really," River said instead.

Their mom made one of her *I don't believe you* faces, which was fair, because River was not acting very believable. For someone so brilliant at not saying the truth, they were not particularly skilled at lying.

They knew their mom was thinking they might be seeing things again but didn't know how to bring it up without upsetting River.

River's mom removed the chair from the door and slid it back into place. River tucked their hands behind their back so they wouldn't shake. As their mom put her hand on the doorknob, they felt their chest constrict.

Their mom threw the door open.

"See, nothing there," she triumphantly said with a smile.

That was because she couldn't see the monster with large red eyes and long thin limbs staring back at them. It swayed from side to side with a low groan, its scaly skin mottled with black fur. It opened its large jaws to reveal at least ten rows of sharp, bloodstained teeth.

River sprang forward to slam the door shut, blocking their mom from the path and the monster from coming through.

"I don't want to look in the closet," River said quickly. "I, uh, spent enough time there."

Their mom crossed her arms. "Is that a joke, or should I be concerned that you're hiding in small spaces?"

"No," River said, "I use the cupboard downstairs for that."

River's mom only frowned a little less. She didn't get River's humor like their dad did. She just grew too worried about everything. River figured it was a mom thing to worry. So they did what they did second best, behind ignoring their monsters.

Distract their mother.

"I'm nervous about going over to Avery's house, and I don't know what to wear." River blurted out the whole statement at once because it wasn't totally a lie.

"Oh, honey, it'll be great," she said, perfectly distracted. "I'm so glad you're making friends. And don't worry. Whatever you wear, you're such a handsome person."

"Okay, Mom," River said, glad not even Pancakes was around to hear their mom talk to them like a little kid. "Give me five minutes to change?"

Their mom walked out of the room with a knowing smile, although River wasn't sure what it was she knew. River didn't go anywhere near the closet, and instead grabbed a pair of shorts and a T-shirt from their dresser that looked good enough. Better that than face that last monster again.

River went to grab their phone from their bed, but it had slid off the edge and onto the floor. Half of the screen was shadowed, partially under the bed.

Their poor heart didn't get the chance to recover from the closet incident before spiking back up to a race River could feel in their throat.

River slowly crept to the edge of the bed and bent to their knees to grab the phone. They had to ignore the slime that they accidentally kneeled in, which was much easier than ignoring the giant bug monster curled up on the underside of their mattress.

Charles reached out a barbed limb, stretching in his slumber. River froze, the edge of the bladed body part a mere inch from their nose. Eyes wide, they forgot how to breathe, only able to focus on the sharpened edge in front of their face.

A few tears leaked, but Charles gave a low, hissing buzz and returned to his original position. River quickly stood up and tried to blink away the tears. They backed up, closer to the door, and sent a quick text to Avery.

Gonna leave now

Avery's response was nearly immediate, and included about seven different animal emojis that didn't make any sense.

Yayayay see you soon!

River felt a little better, although the text affected their heart in a much different way than the monsters did.

They wiped the slime off onto their shorts, making a mental note to keep away from open flames. They'd found out Charles's slime was extremely flammable the hard way: nearly burning the house down when they lit a sage-and-lavender-scented candle in hope of banishing evil forces. (They'd read that burning sage would help but had been limited to what they could find at Target with their mom.)

The only thing it banished was River's ability to get near candles without supervision.

With one look back at the shut closet and the slime trail from under their bed, River walked out of their bedroom.

Maybe an afternoon away would be good for them.

6

The First of Many
Bad Decisions

River didn't want to believe that coming to Avery's house was a mistake, but once they saw the large wooded area behind the houses on Avery's street, they were absolutely convinced it was. It was one of their rules—avoid any woods. Portals loved to open there, probably because it was harder to spot the trees of The Otherwoods in a bunch of regular trees if you didn't know what you were looking for. River was already breaking one rule by getting closer with Avery—would it really be okay to break another one?

"Maybe I should go back home," River said from the passenger seat.

They were already pulled into the Davises' driveway, in

clear sight of the window up front. River's mom turned to look at them with her usual expression of concern.

"River, you're just nervous, it'll be fine."

Those were the exact kind of words someone would say before things became very not fine. Much like going into the woods, it was better to avoid that saying altogether.

But River's mom didn't, and the seed of worry in River's stomach sprouted.

"I don't know, I—"

At that moment, the front door of the house opened, and Avery rushed out to give a wave. Aside from the relief their mom hadn't pulled up at the wrong house, River felt a little sick. Now it was too late to turn back.

"Have fun," River's mom said. "Call me if you need me."

She kissed River on the cheek, in full view of Avery. River's face grew hot, and despite any bad feelings, they couldn't get out of the car fast enough.

"Yeah, okay, 'bye, Mom."

They hopped out onto the driveway and closed the door.

"Love you," their mom said, especially loud.

River's face had to be the exact color of a tomato at this point. Their cheeks felt like River accidentally had lit a candle Charles got some of his slime on. "Love you too," they mumbled.

Thankfully, their mom finally left as River met Avery at the front door.

Avery pulled River in for a hug and, shocked, River only

stiffened. It was a little awkward, but Avery didn't seem to notice. Instead, she gently pushed River inside the house.

"Mom," she called, "River's here!"

Ms. Davis was in the kitchen, standing over a pot bubbling with delicious smells. Her curly black hair was tied back, and she wore a floral apron over her clothes. She looked a lot like Avery, just older, although her brown skin didn't have any of the wrinkles River's mom did.

They certainly wouldn't tell their mom that. Despite the best efforts of The Otherwoods, River did *not* have a death wish.

"Hi, Ms. Davis," River said, squeezing their fingers together. "Thanks for letting me come over. You have a really pretty house."

They hoped they hadn't messed that up. River had never needed to impress anyone's parent before, let alone the parent of a cute girl. That made the stakes seem so much higher.

Ms. Davis smiled brightly, and River thought maybe they got something right.

"Of course, I'm so glad to meet you. You should stay for dinner; it will be ready in a few hours!"

River didn't think they'd ever had a dinner that took more than twenty minutes to make, but whatever Ms. Davis was cooking smelled amazing. Maybe there was something to food that needed a long time.

"Thank you," River said, and immediately wondered if that was enough of an answer. They were pretty sure their parents wouldn't mind if they kept them updated with a text.

"We'll be in the backyard," Avery said, kissing her mom on the cheek. "Let me know if you need help!"

"No worries, love," Ms. Davis said. "You two have fun."

River couldn't even take solace in the fact that Avery was close to her mom and wouldn't find their own mom's behavior that childish. They were too focused on catching up to what Avery had said. *The backyard?*

"Come on." Avery reached out to grab River's hand and lead them through the sliding glass door.

River's heart pounded in their chest, and they weren't sure if it was the fear of the woods, Avery's hand holding theirs, or some weird part of puberty. Maybe it was a combination of all three.

They stepped outside, and River had the urge to squeeze their eyes shut, but they kept them open. It wasn't so bad. The backyard was big, leading all the way up to the edge of the trees. But these trees were different from the trees of The Otherwoods. They were healthy and green, and the sunlight shone through them.

Bad things shouldn't be able to happen on sunny days. Not when only a few lazy clouds drifted through the deep blue of the sky. It was the kind of weather for nice memories.

It made River feel better, like everything would be fine.

They didn't see any spirits or monsters around. Maybe the extra spirits from the day before and the closet portal from earlier were some kind of fluke.

"We can chill here," Avery said, pointing to two chairs set out over a blanket. "I thought it would be nice to be outside, so I brought these from the garage. It feels like summer already, doesn't it?"

River went to take one of the chairs, but Avery sprawled out on the blanket in front of them. River thought sitting over her would be weird, so they joined her on the ground, and tried not to think of all the bugs on the grass. If they saw anything remotely Charles-like, they'd have trouble keeping it together.

Avery turned her face toward River, her cheek pressed against the blanket.

"There's just something so nice about summer. It feels endless, you know?" She smiled. "Almost magical, or spiritual."

River wanted to say that "spiritual" was hardly a compliment in their experience, but that was definitely too weird to get into. They didn't want to immediately scare off Avery by telling her the truth.

"Yeah," River said. "It's nice."

"Plus, no Ms. Deery."

River snorted. "Honestly the best part."

They did understand what Avery meant, though. If there was a good kind of magic in the world, it existed in that moment. With the sun warming their skin, the way their fingers just brushed over the blades of grass, the sky as big as the possibilities of what was next.

There really was something about summer.

Or maybe it was more that there was something about Avery.

"Oh!" Avery pulled out her phone. "I saw this video and thought of you. I wanted to show you."

She pulled up something and angled the screen toward River, close to them so they could both see. The video had a fluffy white cat walking, then suddenly looking off into the distance. It was cute, but why did it make Avery think of River? Is that how River looked to other people when they saw a monster or spirit?

"See? He has your exact color of eyes! Light brown, almost gold." She looked right at River. "They're super pretty."

Now River was even more embarrassed, over both the compliment and for assuming Avery was making fun of them.

"Oh, thanks. That . . . wasn't what I was expecting you to say," River admitted, running their fingers through the grass next to them.

"What were you expecting?"

River focused on the blades of grass. Maybe they shouldn't have said anything at all. They didn't want Avery to remember how strange everyone thought they were. "I . . . I thought you meant because the cat was being weird."

Avery's eyes widened. "What? You're not weird! And even if you are, well, I like weird."

River really felt their cheeks blush then. "Really?"

"Yeah. Can I tell you a secret?" Avery leaned in. "Other than the pansexual thing?"

"If you want," River answered.

"It's embarrassing," Avery warned.

River laughed. "I'm used to embarrassing."

"I can't sleep without my favorite plushie. He's named Señor Mittens Flores-Davis." She looked down, smile a little nervous. "Flores is my mom's maiden name. So he has both her Mexican side and my dad's American side. He's a little gray kitten."

River's jaw practically dropped. "You're kidding."

Avery moaned, gently pushing River. "I told you it was embarrassing!"

"No, no." River laughed over the words. "It's just . . . I have a gray cat, and his name is Mr. Fluffy Pancakes."

Avery's smile was bigger than ever. "No way. Let me see!"

"No problem, my entire phone is pictures of Pancakes." It wasn't a lie. River opened their phone's photo album, which featured the gray tabby from a variety of angles, all around the house.

Avery squealed, scrolling through the photos. "He's so cute. I would do anything for him." She laid back, still looking at the pictures. "Is he chirping at birds here?"

River joined her, pressing their back into the blanket and angling the phone to see the photo in the glare of the clear blue sky. "Oh, yeah. He loves that. I think he's convinced he'll actually catch one through the screen one day."

"I hope I can meet him." Avery sounded almost wistful as she kept looking through the pictures.

River squeezed their fingers, their nerves spiking. It would be easy enough to invite her over. They just had to ask. *You should come over this week after school!*

Simple.

"Ha, yeah," River said instead.

Maybe they weren't quite there yet. But they were with Avery and having a great time. It was a start.

"Smile!" Avery held up River's phone, the camera now open and facing them. River was barely able to adjust as Avery pulled them closer and snapped the selfie. She looked at it, smiling. "Super cute, totally post-worthy." She placed the phone down next to River. "Now we won't forget today."

River didn't think they'd ever forget that day, photo or not.

Avery grabbed River's hand.

"Thanks for coming today," she said. "I wasn't sure you would."

"Me either." The words slipped right out of River's mouth, but Avery only laughed.

"I'm glad you did, though."

"Me too."

In that moment, River was pretty sure they'd do just about anything for Avery.

But in that same moment, a chill washed over River. The kind of chill that only happened when something was very, very wrong. River quickly snapped up, instinct taking over as they looked directly at the woods.

"River?" Avery asked. "Are you okay?"

A portal to The Otherwoods was open. Right in the middle of the shining trees, a hole cut deep, showing only the dark tangled branches River had grown to dread. From the middle of the portal, a long, gray hand stretched.

River forgot how to breathe. "No . . . not now."

They hadn't meant to say the words aloud.

Avery squeezed their hand. "River?" She sounded afraid, but not as afraid as River felt.

What could they have done, though? And they couldn't tell Avery. There was no way she'd believe them.

The clawed, bony hand gripped the grass of the backyard, and the creature pulled itself through the portal. It was gray all over, a sickly gray, and its limbs were tangled, with more joints than necessary. Its skin was pulled tight over its face, and it had veiny yellow eyes and razor-sharp teeth. The monster crawled on all fours and, despite the ghoulish appearance, moved quickly.

It looked directly at them and started to sprint toward Avery.

And for only the second time in their twelve and a half years, River made an awful mistake.

They locked eyes with the monster.

The monster stopped, only a few feet away. Fear coursed through River's body as the monster looked right back at them. Seeing them. River was frozen. River was out in the open, not ignoring the monster, but staring at it head-on.

The monster's thin lips curled up into a smile.

7

The Worst
Possible Outcome

River didn't know what to do. Unfortunately, they had only prepared for hanging out with a new friend, not for a potential monster attack.

"You're acting really weird," Avery said. "I'm getting freaked out."

River tore their eyes away from the monster for only a moment and took in Avery's expression. It was the first time they had felt something like heartbreak, seeing the way Avery looked at them. Not like something was wrong with the situation, but like something was wrong with River.

They didn't want to admit it, but they often wondered that too.

It was so easy to be with her, but none of that mattered when she gave them the same look everyone else did. She wouldn't believe them.

And that hurt.

But River had to do something.

The hairs on the back of River's neck rose as the muscles of the monster's hind legs twitched under its papery skin. River looked at Avery with wild eyes. "Run."

Avery didn't seem to understand and showed more concern than absolute fear for her life, but she still ran toward the rear of the house with River. Almost at the door, River turned back to see if the monster was close.

River learned in that moment that turning back while running for your life is a horrible idea.

The monster leapt into the air, a shadow falling over them. It quickly soared across the yard and landed in front of them with a loud thump. River stopped automatically at the sight of the monster blocking the way. Since Avery couldn't see it, she kept going.

And slammed right into the monster, then fell back onto the grass.

Avery's shocked expression matched River's own thoughts. River had looked at the monster, and now it could touch them, just like the birdlike monster had (almost) done all those years ago. Only Avery couldn't see it, which had to make it more terrifying.

"I . . . What?" Avery said from the ground.

River couldn't waste time answering. They ran to Avery and yanked her up to her feet, then pulled Avery into a run.

The monster lashed out, two claws digging into River's arm. River yelped in pain but ran through the tears.

This time, they didn't look back.

Instead, hand in hand, River and Avery ran in the direction of the woods. Doing so filled River with a strong sense of dread, but it was difficult to think logically while being chased by a giant monster with deadly teeth and claws.

River didn't know how long they'd been running when the two stopped for breath behind a large tree. River peered around the trunk, but they no longer could see the monster. It wasn't a total relief—if it wasn't right behind them, where was it?

"What's going on? Did I run into something?" Avery's voice was a cross between a whisper and a yell, muted but with a yell's intensity. "Is your arm okay?"

River looked down at their arm, the stinging less noticeable with the adrenaline of running away. Two jagged cuts tore through the skin, starting halfway up their forearm and ending at their wrist. The cuts weren't deep, but the trails of blood staining their fingers and dropping to the ground below made things look worse.

They also made River feel a lot worse, and a little dizzy.

"I'm okay," River said, although they were certainly not okay. "And we're being attacked by a monster."

Their breath caught as they prepared for the worst reaction. Their eyes stung.

Avery looked like she wanted to flat-out reject that idea, but her eyes were drawn to River's bleeding arm. "I didn't see anything."

River gave a pained smile. "Most people don't."

Avery dropped her jaw. "And you always have?"

River nodded.

"Well, shiitake mushrooms," Avery said. "That's not good."

Her arm trembled against the bark of the tree, but other than that, she was taking it incredibly well.

"You believe me?" River asked.

Of all the unexplainable things they had encountered in their lifetime, this was one they had never accounted for.

"I have to," Avery answered, "because I don't know how else to explain *that*." She pointed to the wound on River's arm, which was indeed very monster-like. There was nothing visible to Avery that could've caused such a mark, so they were already limited on reasonable explanations.

River could hardly believe it. Someone was taking them seriously—*Avery* was taking them seriously. They weren't facing it by themself anymore.

Despite everything, it brought the dragonflies back, buzzing around in their stomach on top of the anxiety and fear still present.

"What does the monster want?" Avery asked.

"To take us through a portal into a scary monster world," River answered automatically. "At least, I'm pretty sure that's it."

Avery bit her lip. "Oh, that's all? Wonderful." She squeezed her hand, perhaps to stop some of the shaking. "So, what do we do?"

That was a question River didn't have an answer to.

They were so frustrated, they could cry. But they didn't want to do that in front of Avery of all people.

Still, why did things have to change suddenly, with the monsters growing more dangerous? Couldn't River have gotten *one* nice day with a friend?

It really wasn't fair.

But they weren't alone, and that was something. A major something.

"We should try to get back inside," River said. "Can you call your mom for help?"

Avery's eyes widened. "I left my phone back there."

River checked their own pocket, only to wince. "Me too."

"I guess we can run back screaming?"

River didn't get the chance to weigh the options and respond, because a veiny gray hand reached down between their heads and claws pulled back up on the bark, leaving deep cuts in the trunk. River's heart pounded as they slowly looked up to see the monster reaching down from a large branch, poised to strike. Avery looked up too, sensing River's panic, and spotted the marks left in the bark.

So they ran back screaming.

The monster flew through the trees above them, chasing after Avery and River. It threw itself from branch to branch, moving nearly as quickly as the two of them giving their all below. Finally, they broke through the denser wooded area and into Avery's backyard.

The glass door of Avery's house slid open, and Ms. Davis stood there.

"What is going on?" she demanded, a very mom-like mix of worried and annoyed.

Avery and River were too focused on running toward her to attempt to explain. River's chest burned, and they felt a little like throwing up.

Then Avery cried out.

Ms. Davis started toward them as River turned around to Avery, fallen on the grass. The monster slowed down, then stood right over her, its large mouth dropped open to reveal every pointed tooth.

River was frozen.

The monster picked up Avery, closing its limb around her tightly. To her and Ms. Davis, she must have appeared to be floating in midair. She screamed; Ms. Davis screamed. River might have screamed too, but they couldn't tell. The world seemed to move in slow motion, and their body felt heavy and numb.

Holding on to Avery, the monster ran toward the portal.

No, no, no!

Yet River couldn't move. The fear, the hopelessness of the situation, gripped them like vines. All River could do was watch.

Avery strained to hold out her hand in River's direction, but she was already too far. River only stared at her with frightened eyes as the monster pulled her through the portal.

It closed around them, and only then was River able to

move. They sprinted toward where the portal had been, but their frantic hands grasped only air.

Ms. Davis caught up to them, voice lined with worry and terror, calling out for her daughter.

River looked up, and the worst was confirmed.

Avery was gone.

8

The Missing Girl

The time after Avery's disappearance was a blur of flashing lights and loud voices. It was so far away from the afternoon spent together, fingertips touching, only birds and the occasional speeding car making noise. With the police, ambulances, and so many people gathered, the world felt all too real.

River wasn't used to things feeling so grounded, and it was as horrible as the otherworldly elements they were used to.

Nobody understood what had happened, not even Ms. Davis, and she was there. River's arm was sliced and Avery had vanished into thin air. As much as Ms. Davis was questioned, and as much as authorities tried to draw conclusions, nothing added up. The facts were things that simply couldn't occur, so the authorities had to supply alternatives that could.

They didn't realize that sometimes eyes can't tell the whole story. At least, not in the way they needed to.

The reasonable explanation that most people decided on was that Avery and River had been playing in the woods when a tree branch slashed River. It must have been quite the tree branch to leave a mark like that, but nobody allowed themselves to make that comment, because they continued with their version of events. Avery got scared and ran off into the woods, then got lost. Ms. Davis simply *imagined* that Avery returned with River, because brains can't be trusted when filled with worry and fear.

River might have agreed with that last part a little, but certainly not in the case of what Ms. Davis saw.

River couldn't say much. Avery may have believed them about monsters, but Avery was gone. River knew the police and paramedics wouldn't offer them the same support. Nobody seemed to mind that River didn't talk. They chalked it up to River being a scared, shy middle schooler. A fair assumption, not very off base.

In other circumstances, River might've gotten annoyed they were being treated like a little kid.

But these were not other circumstances. They were the worst, most unfortunate ones, and River felt helpless. They just wanted to bury their face in Pancakes' fur and cry.

Instead, they were sitting in the back of an ambulance, where a paramedic finished bandaging up their arm.

Luckily, when the blood and dirt was cleaned out, the wound didn't look that bad, not even needing stitches. It really hurt, but as long as River kept it clean and changed the bandages, the man assured River, they would indeed survive.

"You're a brave kid," he said. "That must've hurt."

"Yeah," River said, wishing people would stop calling them brave.

Brave people didn't freeze up when their friends needed them.

The paramedic turned to River's mom, who stood next to them. River couldn't have paid attention to the words spoken if they wanted to. Nothing felt right. Their senses were all in overdrive. The world around them looked too sharp, sounded too loud. Their eyes were scratchy with the need to cry, and they wanted to scream or puke or run away or cause some damage. Maybe all of the above, if it was possible.

It was a similar feeling to the power people held over River when they misgendered them. They wanted to jump right out of their own skin.

River looked at their bandaged arm. The wrap was kind of like what boxers wore, although it mostly covered River's forearm and not their hand. It hurt, but in a more manageable way. Their eyes moved past the gauze, to the open ambulance door and the chaos outside.

A bunch of people from the neighborhood had gathered to look for Avery. River saw their dad take an orange vest and get ready to go out into the woods. There were plenty of people, and some intimidating police dogs, ready for the search.

"River?" They jumped at the sound of the voice, before turning to meet their mother's eyes, rimmed in red and shadowed underneath. "Let's get you home, okay?"

River nodded. They wouldn't be much help there anyway.

They didn't know how much help they'd be at all. More than they ever had before, River desperately wished they were someone else.

They took their mom's hand, said a thank-you and goodbye to the paramedic, and followed their mom through the crowd of people. They didn't see Mr. or Ms. Davis anywhere, but plenty of the people they walked past looked at River. The expressions on their faces were difficult to read in the dying light.

Did they feel bad for them? Did they think River was just weird?

Did they blame them?

River didn't mind if they did. They blamed themself.

And hate boiled in them, directly inward. Avery needed someone braver, someone stronger, someone who didn't want to run away and cry.

But the only chance she had was them. The person who got her kidnapped in the first place.

Finally getting past the crowds of eyes, River and their mom made it to the road. With night falling, the hollowness in River grew. What if more monsters came at night? Would they be able to hurt the people searching?

Or was it just River they wanted?

As the car pulled away, River stared out the window. The people in brightly colored vests started pouring into the woods. River shivered at the way the dark trees swallowed them up, like a warning of what would come.

"Don't worry," River's mom said. "They'll find her."

River didn't answer, so that they wouldn't have to lie. They knew that no one would find Avery in those woods, because she wasn't there.

She was in The Otherwoods. And the only person who could find her was River.

And even though they were more scared than they'd ever been, they knew they would have to try.

9

The Reluctant Adventurer

If River had been a real hero, they would have opened the closet portal to The Otherwoods and gone after Avery the second they got home. Instead, they'd been hiding under their blanket for close to an hour. They wanted to be buried under it and never have to resurface. They felt numb, stuck, like they were sinking underwater despite being firmly on land. Their eyes stung, but they didn't cry.

A knock sounded on the door. "River?" their mom asked.

That was a sure sign that things were terrible. Since when did their mom knock?

She seemed to sense that a response wouldn't come,

because she slowly cracked open the door, filling the room with light, and slipped inside.

Her voice was soft and gentle. "I have some dinner for you. You should eat something."

They didn't move to look up at her. "I'm not hungry."

"Just a snack? Your dad made some cookies earlier, you can have a few this once, I'll get you some."

"Mom. I'm fine."

"Something to drink, then? I'll get water, you want ice?"

River sat up in bed, their face heating as a tear chose the absolute worst instant to fall. "Mom! Can you just leave me alone?" Both of them froze at River's raised voice. River wasn't the type to yell, and it seemed to echo through the dark bedroom. "I . . . I just need to be by myself a little."

Their mom took a moment to respond, clearing her throat. "Okay, love. I'm outside if you need anything."

It annoyed River slightly that she was still pushing, but they swallowed it back. Their parents probably didn't know what to do in such a situation either. "Is Dad still out looking?"

Their mom nodded. "They'll find her, River."

"What if they don't?" River asked.

Her lips twisted and her wet eyes shimmered. "I guess we can't think about that, because they have to." She paused. "Are you okay in here alone?"

River nodded.

Maybe they weren't, but their mom was right about one

63

thing: it wasn't worth thinking about, because they had to find Avery.

"Let me know if you get hungry. Or . . . well, you know." Their mom's mouth curled slightly upward in a shape far too sad to call a smile.

"Thanks," River said.

She stepped out of the room with the untouched plate of food. River fell back onto their sheets as the door creaked to a close. Their eyes started to water, but they just put their head into their pillow.

What had they done?

They knew it was dangerous to get close to someone, but they'd done it anyway. Now Avery was gone, and it was all their fault. If River couldn't save her before, what made them think they could save her now?

"Mmrrrow?" Pancakes leapt onto the bed, accidentally stepping on River's phone. It lit up bright, cutting through the shadows, and opened to where it had last been used.

The photos app, displaying the picture of River and Avery. Both of them had huge smiles on their faces. In the photo, Avery's arm was around River. Her sparkling dark brown eyes held the sun as they looked right into the camera. Next to her, River seemed to have swallowed a little bit of that sunshine too.

They looked happy. Happier than River could remember feeling before that moment.

River bit their bottom lip until it hurt. Avery had been there for them, even when they made it difficult. She'd believed them when they told her about the monsters. She was the first person to see all of River and accept them, and they'd let her go.

River wiped at their face. No matter how much River had pushed others away and kept to themself, Avery hadn't given up on them.

So no matter what, they couldn't give up on her.

While River's knowledge of preparing for survival didn't help them when packing for a friend's house, it did help them when packing for a rescue mission. River filled their backpack with all the necessities they thought of: rope, pocket knife, water, snacks, first aid kit, lighter and backup matches, deodorant, to-go toilet paper and bathroom wipes, because River was not about to wipe their butt with leaves . . . all the important things.

It was heavy, but with both straps over their shoulders, they could manage the weight. River dressed as comfortably as possible—sweatpants, a T-shirt, and a zip-up hoodie in case it got cold. They didn't know when they would be able to change, but their bag would only fit one emergency pair of underwear.

The Otherwoods was scary enough that peeing their pants was a legitimate concern, and showers were probably not an option.

"Okay," River said to no one. "That's everything."

They reached for the backpack with a shaking hand, then froze. They crumpled to the side of their bed, burying their face in the bedspread with a groan.

They couldn't do it. They couldn't go.

Since making the decision to go after Avery, they'd tried to focus only on that and the methodical packing. But with everything all together, they felt their breathing quicken. Packing for a rescue mission was one thing. Actually going on it was another.

What would they do if they ran out of food? Water? What if they peed their pants *twice* and didn't have another spare pair? What if a monster got them? What if they were already too late?

River's breaths grew too fast as panic rose in them. Their head spun, and they felt like pulling on their hair or their clothes.

No, she's okay, please, she's okay.

They took a deep, shaky breath and got back on their feet.

Maybe they were hopeless, and maybe it was a terrible idea. But River still had to try, because they were all Avery had. So even if they were on the verge of a panic attack and most certainly setting themself up for failure, they would go.

Into The Otherwoods.

"I'm going to do this, Pancakes," River said. "I'm going to get her back."

Pancakes blinked slowly. Which they hoped was Cat for *Yes, you most definitely will!*

River picked up their backpack and secured it around their shoulders. They clipped the extra strap around their waist.

"Do you think the portal is still there?" River gestured to the closet, where the chair once again blocked the handle.

Pancakes, being a cat, didn't have an opinion on the topic, but River was nearly sure it was. The Otherwoods had wanted them this entire time. They must have taken Avery for that reason. Which meant that whoever, or whatever, was behind this knew River would follow.

River leaned over Pancakes and gave him a kiss on the head.

"I love you, Mr. Fluffy Pancakes," River said.

Sure, the full name was embarrassing, but people are allowed to be embarrassing when they might be seeing someone they love for the last time.

Pancakes licked River's nose. His scratchy tongue was uncomfortable since it was meant for grooming fur and not goose bump–covered skin, but River appreciated the thought.

With that carrying them forward, River took a deep breath and crossed the room. They removed the chair from the closet door. Their heart pounded in their throat. The door seemed silent, nothing banging up against it. That was a small relief, but something.

River reached for the handle and slowly turned it.

Still nothing.

The little voice in their head told them it was a terrible idea and they should give up now. River opened the closet door.

It was still there, a large entrance to The Otherwoods, the other side of the doorframe filled with trees and strange sounds. Portals didn't usually last this long, but nothing was usual about the situation. Maybe The Otherwoods somehow knew that day was different.

Behind them, Pancakes hissed.

River spun around to see Pancakes, now on all fours and bristled, staring at Charles, who was halfway out from underneath the bed. Charles gave his buzzing hiss, one bladed limb dug into the mattress to hold his upper body upright. He blinked at River.

For the first time, River looked back at him. It was terrifying, but River figured they would simply have to adjust to terrifying things.

"I'm going in," River told Charles. "So please don't kill me."

River wasn't sure that Charles would be able to understand them. Charles buzzed, slime dripping from his pincers. He looked past River at The Otherwoods behind them before returning his eyes to River.

River gulped. They were glad Charles wasn't standing at full height.

"You're from there, aren't you?" River asked. "Any advice?"

It was a long shot, but River was desperate. Charles was scary, but at least he was familiar. River had no idea what they were about to walk into.

Charles kept looking into River's eyes for a while, probably too long. It made River's skin crawl, but they managed to not tear away from his gaze. Finally, Charles pointed one sharp limb in the direction of Pancakes.

"I should take Pancakes?" River asked.

It was possible the monster was asking permission to eat Pancakes, but River thought they could be an optimist this once.

Charles blinked, a bit of slime from his spiked limb dripping onto the bed.

Pancakes—afraid, disgusted, or some combination of the two—hopped right off the bed and crossed the floor. He rubbed around River's legs and looked lazily in the direction of The Otherwoods.

Maybe Charles was right. River could barely stomach being alone with Charles under their bed; how would they make it through The Otherwoods by themself? It was possible cats were good to have in supernatural situations. Pancakes was the only other being that was able to see what River saw.

The Otherwoods in front of them didn't seem to have any immediate monsters, but the silence was almost scarier. River looked back down at Pancakes.

"You sure you want to come?"

Pancakes responded by hissing at Charles. Which, in some way, was an answer. River figured they had enough water and packets of tuna to keep Pancakes happy. Plus, he wouldn't care about peeing in the dirt.

And it was probably better than leaving him alone with Charles.

River took one last look at their bedroom, wondering if this would really be the last time they saw it. They tried to commit every detail to memory. The overstocked bookshelves, the giant poster of Eevee and all the Eeveelutions hanging on the wall (a very nonbinary- and trans-friendly Pokémon, River thought), the bright blue comforter that River's grandmother had bought for them.

Charles, the freakish monster that lived under the bed.

"Thanks, Charles," River said.

The bug monster drooled more flammable slime, then clicked his pincers twice.

Maybe that was some kind of goodbye. River didn't know whether to be moved by the sudden strange connection or terrified. If Charles wasn't so bad, what would they have to face in The Otherwoods that *was*?

River gulped, and sniffed back tears.

"You ready?" River asked Pancakes.

Pancakes lightly nipped their leg. A call to action if River had ever seen one.

We're coming, Avery, River thought.

Swallowing the need to cry, desperately hoping things would turn out okay, and with Pancakes by their side, River crossed through the portal.

10

The Endless Otherwoods

The air shifted around River as they stepped into The Otherwoods. There was a constant chill to it that wasn't entirely unpleasant, just a little bit off. It wasn't suffocating, but felt fresh, like it was untouched by anything human. A smell hit their nose that was wet, mossy, with the slightest hint of rust. River's shoe crunched against fallen leaves and twigs. In front of them, past the gray fog, were the bent trees in shades of black, dark gray, and blue. As River stepped forward, the trees almost reached toward them. They seemed to buzz, a strange welcome to this new place.

At their side, Pancakes sniffed the ground. He walked a few feet away from River, checking out the tree trunks and grayed plants sprouting from the dirt. But Pancakes didn't go far, which was a small relief to River. They hoped he would stay close.

River turned around, still wanting to hang on to the safety of their home nearby.

But the portal was gone. Behind them, the woods seemed to stretch on forever, the way it did in every other direction. There was no trace of the closet door, or River's bedroom, or even Charles. Only the gnarled branches that bent toward River, reaching out with little snaps and cracks.

River swallowed.

There was no going back.

It gave them an empty, hollow feeling, somehow mixed with heaviness in their stomach. Like everything in their chest had sunk down. What if they couldn't find a portal back? How long would they be there?

Oh God, what would their *parents* think?

River imagined their mom and dad entering the bedroom to find them and Pancakes missing. Their chest hurt at the thought of the fear and sadness their parents would feel. Would everyone start searching for them, too?

River blinked. They couldn't be found anyway. It was up to them to find Avery and get back home. They had to keep going. And quickly. Avery must have been terrified, suddenly being in a strange place. River had some preparation, as little as they believed it'd help them, but everything about the world was new to Avery. It would be better once River found her.

But how?

River looked for a sign of anything around them, but

there wasn't much. Only the foggy view of the forest, the dark, twisted trees with the occasional frightening red stain, and the dirt holding it all together.

Unsure if they'd be able to hold themself together for long, River turned to Pancakes, who was gnawing on a piece of yellowed grass.

"Okay, here's the plan," River said to Pancakes, trying to keep their voice tremble-free. "We move directly ahead, looking for any signs of water. The monsters would need to drink, so they probably live around there. If we follow the monsters, we can find Avery?"

Even they could tell how unsure they sounded.

Being a cat, Pancakes did not answer or care about River's uncertainty. When River walked a few steps forward, Pancakes followed. River didn't know if it was the familiarity of their scent in an unfamiliar world, or if Pancakes was as scared as they were. Maybe there was some unspoken interspecies communication between them.

It didn't seem likely, but weirder things had happened. Like entering an entirely different world through a portal in their closet.

Or maybe, just maybe, it was some kind of magic.

River didn't want to admit it, but they almost thought they could feel it in the air. That low buzz, almost too quiet to notice, but filled with life. Filled with energy. Compelling them forward. In the way the branches swayed toward them. The ground seemed to brighten up a bit with each step.

River wanted to ignore that call and turn back. It's what they did best. But they didn't have much of a choice.

Forward was as good a direction as any, so River and Pancakes moved that way.

With the seemingly endless trees stretched out in front of them, River didn't know how they would find water, let alone Avery. As the two padded along for what felt like an hour with no signs of anything, River's worry inflated like a balloon.

River's foot caught on a fallen branch, and they lurched forward. River balanced themself on a tree, forgetting about their bandaged arm. Pain shot up to their shoulder, and the wound burned. The bark around their hand turned a brilliant shade of blue, but when River pulled back, it immediately disappeared.

River didn't like the idea of strange, color-changing trees. They also didn't like the sharp soreness that ran up their arm.

As River gripped the bandage in an attempt to stifle the pain, the balloon of their worries popped. All their anxiety and frustration and fear poured out of them. Their skin itched, and they suddenly wished they could step out of it. They wished they could be someone else. Someone stronger, who didn't freeze and cry when things went wrong.

Then Avery would have a chance of being saved.

River slid down the tree trunk and sat on a gnarled root, backpack pushed into the bark. They dropped their head into their arms to shut out the strange world for a moment.

River had rushed into this. They had no business being in The Otherwoods and trying to save anyone. They would've been better off giving up. If they could even find their way home now.

But Avery was here.

Little paws pressed up River's legs, and a small wet nose and whiskers tickled their forehead. They opened their eyes to see the face of Pancakes blocking their vision. Pancakes meowed loudly.

If there was one thing River could count on, at the darkest of times, it was Pancakes letting them know when he was hungry.

"Sorry, Pancakes. I'll get you a snack."

Not wanting to use too much food, River tore open a pouch of tuna and split pieces between themself and Pancakes. Plain chunk white tuna wasn't exactly a favorite of River's, but they didn't expect fine dining in The Otherwoods. Survival sometimes called for plain tuna. River poured some of their water into the lid of the bottle and let Pancakes lap it up. They took a cautious sip and finished what Pancakes hadn't.

Again, desperate times.

At least the thought of drinking after their cat distracted them from the hopelessness of before. It was a small silver lining to an unfortunately fishy situation. Full from the tuna, Pancakes was resting on top of River.

Feeling slightly better, River pushed against the tree to sit up. The bark glowed that uncanny blue, like something impossible was shimmering under the surface. When River moved away, the light disappeared and the tree returned to the normal dull bark in shades of gray and brown.

"That's a little weird . . ."

Pancakes looked over at River, possibly in agreement, possibly to ask for more tuna.

Taking that as a yes, River scooped up Pancakes with their good arm and got to their feet. They gently guided one of Pancakes' paws to the bark of the tree, but when the soft pads met the bark, nothing happened. With the slightest touch from River, the tree glowed, but Pancakes didn't produce the same reaction.

Did the trees of The Otherwoods only react to humans?

The hairs on River's arms stood as they wondered why the trees glowed at all. It was another reminder of how far they were from home, and probably good reason to keep going. River knelt to set Pancakes down, but the cat meowed in protest.

River rolled their eyes. "Fine, I'll carry you, but only for a little."

Pancakes wouldn't understand anyway, but River was actually glad to have the cat to hold on to. It was someone familiar in a place that was anything but.

River walked forward, trying not to make too much noise, even with Pancakes' extra weight. They were still surrounded by the dense trees, branches intertwining and creating a net separating them from the sky, but the short break had given River a bit more energy.

A spark of hope that in the next block of trees, there would be something worth finding.

Or . . . the next.

River had gone through five more disappointingly empty tree blocks when they saw it. A small pool of water. Hope blossomed within them. Water meant life. Monsters would be nearby, and that meant Avery could be close too.

They rushed over to the pool of water and quickly refilled their aluminum bottle, choosing to believe it was safe to drink and not thinking of the alternative. All they had to do was look for some sign of Avery. They replaced the water bottle in their backpack, picked up Pancakes again, and checked around the bases of trees for tracks in the dirt.

After a few steps, a drop smacked against River's forehead.

Maybe rain was common in The Otherwoods. They didn't know how weather worked there.

River looked up to check for dark clouds, and their stomach turned to stone. They involuntarily squeezed Pancakes a little bit tighter.

A yard above their heads, a huge monster nestled in the branches. A cross between an owl and an alligator but completely gray, the beast had a big pointed beak rimmed with teeth. Its skin was scaly in some places and feathered in others, and there were long red scars running up its back. Giant wings rested on either side of its large body, and a spiked tail dropped to its left. Under pointed horns at the top of its head, its eyes were closed.

River realized that looking for an area with monsters nearby perhaps wasn't the best idea, and was something they should've better thought through.

If the creature was asleep, maybe they'd have a chance of getting away safely.

Pancakes growled, and the monster twitched, moving its massive claws.

Well. So much for that.

11

The Monster in the Trees

River's own legs twitched, muscles getting ready to run. But River was stuck, breath caught in their throat. The monster nestled back into the branch, eyes closed. There was still a chance. They had to get far away from the monster without making a single sound. With a nervous cat in their arms and a rough forest floor.

Easy, right?

Sucking in air slowly, River took their first step, their entire body tensed. They tried to keep Pancakes close to them, hoping that if another growl escaped from his throat, it wouldn't be enough to wake the monster.

Of course it had to have feathers—the one thing that Pancakes couldn't resist. River could sense Pancakes' predator instincts tingling. Even with River holding him tight, Pancakes was ready to pounce. They had to get out of there fast.

River's foot fell onto the ground without making a noise. So far, so good. They took another step, and another, all of them light and silent. Maybe River would actually make it away from this monster unnoticed.

A twig snapped under their foot.

The monster looked down immediately, meeting River's eyes.

Or maybe they'd die.

River's mind didn't have time to think about running—their body just did it. It was awkward with Pancakes in their arms and the backpack on their shoulders, but they ran as fast as they could. The trees blurred as River darted around them. The world was shaky, and Pancakes started to squirm, so they gripped him tighter.

They had a bit more experience in running away from horrible monsters at this point, so they didn't look back. They didn't think of anything at all except getting away. Of course, they weren't *that* experienced. And it didn't seem like running away from deadly monsters was something one could grow used to. Fear still rippled through their body. Between the air stinging their lungs because of overuse and their chest already tight with worry, River considered the very real possibility that they would pass out before the monster caught them.

The monster cawed from behind, a metallic, choked sound. River ran faster, but they could tell the monster was right on their heels, snapping down branches that were in its way.

River was pushed forward. Pancakes flew out of their arms and twisted in the air to land on his feet. River wasn't so lucky, crashing face-first into the twigs and leaves. They couldn't feel the many scrapes now on their body or the reopened wound on their arm. They dug their fingers in the dirt to pull themself up and forward as quick as they could.

Pancakes hissed in front of them as something tugged on River's ankle. They fell back on their belly, knocking the air out of them, and let out a strangled scream. Being quiet didn't matter anymore. They managed to twist onto their back and tuck their legs out of reach.

Turning around, however, was a mistake.

River was now face-to-face with the monster. Its open jaw revealed the sharp line of stained teeth on each end of its beak. Its talons were dug into the ground, its tail swung high, and the massive wings were unfurled. It overshadowed River entirely. The monster released another screech before poising itself to strike.

River could only stare at the teeth that would certainly tear apart their skin.

The creature pounced just as a round ball of fur flew from behind River. Pancakes landed on River's chest and hissed at the monster, the cat's ears bent all the way back and tail puffy.

The monster's jaws snapped shut. Its eyes narrowed. It leaned in, almost curiously.

River watched the standoff between feline and ferocious monster with their heart in their throat. River was no stranger to weird things, but the sight in front of them was perhaps the weirdest of all.

The moment was tense, a stare-down between the looming monster and the fluffy cat.

Then Pancakes smacked the creature's face, scratching it right in its eye. It reared back and gave a painful screech. With one eye still working, it lifted its head to crash its pointed beak onto Pancakes, but a branch smashed down on the head of the beast.

Dark blood dripped from its eye, and possibly finding the potential lunch not worth the effort, it flapped its large wings and took off.

As confused as they were relieved, River looked to the other end of the branch, which was held by a teenager. He was white, but even more than River, with skin that seemed like the sunlight had never grazed it. His thick black hair fell to his chin on one side but was shaved on the other. With his brown leather jacket, he kind of looked like a character from a video game.

River grabbed Pancakes and pulled him close. While Pancakes was already on the list of things River loved most, they hadn't realized how tough the cat was. River was glad Pancakes had come with them. They hadn't expected to battle monsters, and if they had been alone, they probably wouldn't have made it past the first one.

But who was this high schooler, and how were they there in the first place?

River looked over at him. The boy smiled, dropping the bloody branch in a move that River thought seemed incredibly heroic.

"First time in The Otherwoods?" he asked. "Smart of you to bring a cat."

12

The Wayward Spirit

River didn't know what to say. Frankly, they hadn't been expecting to see another person. "It was?" was what came out.

"You didn't know?" The boy raised an eyebrow. "You're sure lucky, then. Cats are one of the few species that can see monsters and spirits. And spirits can't possess you if a cat is in possession of you."

"Don't you mean if I'm in possession of a cat?" River asked.

The boy laughed, before turning to Pancakes in a *can-you-believe-this-kid* kind of way. "Right, sure." He gave Pancakes another knowing look. "You got quite the kid here."

Pancakes didn't look all that amused.

River wasn't sure what was more unnerving, the fact that another monster could pop up at any moment, or this guy.

"Um . . . he's a cat?" River wiped some dirt off themself. "He can't understand you."

"He can't understand you, *human*," the boy said. "We, on the other hand, have a connection." Pancakes growled at him. "A budding one."

River blinked. The boy looked human. He had human eyes and human ears and arms and legs. He certainly didn't look anything like the monsters.

"You're a spirit?" River asked.

"No, I'm a tree," the boy said sarcastically.

River rolled their eyes. "The spirits I've seen have been more . . . translucent. You just look like a regular human."

The boy crossed his arms. "That's because you've only seen spirits in your world, where we fade if we spend too much time before passing on. Here, we have more power." The boy stepped toward River, reaching out a hand. River went to take it, and when they clasped hands, the boy's skin grew more translucent. "Can't maintain it with contact, though."

He pulled River to their feet, and River brushed off the rest of the dirt. "Thanks." River eyed the spirit. "Why do you have more power here?"

River thought that The Otherwoods was for monsters. Most of the spirits that mentioned it back home seemed to fear the place as much as River did.

"Well, I'm not a superhero, but of course I'll do better in a spirit realm than in the realm of the living. That's common sense."

River's jaw dropped. *A* spirit realm? "There are more of them?"

"Sure." The spirit looked at River like they were joking. "There are two: The Otherwoods and The Elsewhere. Obviously."

River didn't think it was all that obvious, but the spirit went on.

"I never expected to see an actual human here," the boy said. He started to walk around River, eyeing them curiously. "I've heard about living humans with some magic who can travel here . . . but it's apparently been a long time since one has. There are spirits that have been here for over a decade and never met one—I almost didn't believe it. Didn't think any human would have the guts to come here." The boy bent over to be eye level with River. "Especially not one so . . . small." He frowned. "What are you, eight?"

River was getting annoyed with this spirit. "I'm *twelve*."

"Huh." The spirit looked them up and down like they were adjusting their calculations. "Well, good for you, man. Um, I mean, girl. Person?"

"I'm nonbinary," River said quietly.

They hadn't expected coming out to a random spirit to be another scary aspect of The Otherwoods, but at least it was a more familiar fear.

"Cool," the spirit said. "I think I've heard of that."

River opened their mouth and closed it again. That was not the usual response they got. Most of the other kids at school were very familiar with the term, although River wasn't sure if that was because of having a classmate like them.

"It means I'm not a boy or a girl. I'm just River."

"You're a river?" the boy asked, visibly confused.

"No, no, my *name* is River."

"Oh, okay. You're not a boy or a girl, you're just a person," the spirit said. "Well, a person who can see monsters and ghosts."

That pretty much summed it up.

"Yeah," River said. "Exactly."

"Well, nice to meet you, kid," the spirit said. "My name's Xavier. I'm pretty sure I had a last name too. Maybe two? I don't know, life details get all fuzzy after you die."

River gulped. That was kind of scary. They had to keep that piece of information at a distance, or the panic would rise up in them again.

"How did you die?" River asked. Not exactly a great subject change, but at least Xavier was still alive in some sense?

"How rude, asking a spirit how he died when we only just met."

"I'm sorry, I—"

"Nah, it's fine. But don't go around asking all spirits! Some really don't like it." Xavier put his finger to his chin. "Let's see . . . death, death, hmm . . ." His face lit up. "Right! I was hit by a car when I was biking home from school. Very sudden, super tragic. You should have seen my funeral. So many flowers, the church was like a florist's. I was practically a celebrity. People gave great speeches, not a dry eye in the place."

Xavier seemed rather pleased with his death. River

thought that was a strange attitude, but they supposed it was better than being sad about it.

"That's . . . nice?" River said. "How old were—um, are you?"

"I was fifteen when I died, so I suppose I'm still fifteen now. I've just been fifteen for two years. I think. Time's a little weird here. Regardless, it's hard to feel at least seventeen when I haven't aged. Hard to mature when you aren't living."

Seventeen? That was a whole adult! Sure, Xavier might be more like fifteen plus two or so, but even fifteen seemed so much older than River. By fifteen, River would be learning to drive, going out with friends all the time, maybe going on dates . . .

Or they'd be dead in The Otherwoods.

"But I'm being rude, what's the cat's name?" Xavier asked.

River was not about to admit to a teenager that they'd named their cat Mr. Fluffy Pancakes. The actual name was bad enough. Poor Pancakes. They should have named him something cool and intimidating, like Blade or Lightning. But it wasn't like River could change it now. What if Xavier really could talk to cats, and caught River in the lie? "His name is Pancakes," River said.

"Hello, Pancakes." Xavier smiled. "Excellent smack to the monster. I was impressed."

"Thanks again for that," River added. "You really saved us."

"Pancakes had it covered, but happy to help." Xavier gave another questioning look at River. "What are you doing in The Otherwoods anyway? This place isn't exactly human-friendly. Aren't you scared?"

River was absolutely scared and very much wanted to go home, but they weren't about to admit that either. "I'm here to save my friend," River said, puffing out their chest to seem more heroic than they sounded. "A monster took her." They didn't know how to form the right words, but maybe the spirit would be able to help. "Have you seen or heard anything about it? Do you know where they might have taken her?"

"I didn't see or hear anything, but they probably took her to The Centertrees. Tough break." Xavier had a pained expression on his face. "Well, nice meeting you. Maybe I'll see you as a spirit, come say hey." Xavier turned and started walking away.

"Wait!" River grabbed his arm. Xavier turned to look at River, his leather-covered arm translucent to the touch. "What are The Centertrees? How do I get there?"

Xavier gaped like a fish. "What are The Cen— Don't you know anything about The Otherwoods?"

River didn't know what to say to that. They'd spent their whole life trying to ignore The Otherwoods—pretend it didn't exist. And besides, it wasn't like there was a book for them to check out on the subject.

They hadn't realized it was a spirit realm, or known there was another spirit realm out there too. How were they supposed to know about specific places inside it?

Xavier rolled his eyes when River didn't respond, but explained, "The Centertrees are the source of magic in The

Otherwoods. They're what keeps this whole place alive! It's right in the middle of monster territory, so of course, they bring all their prey there."

"*Prey?*" Were the monsters going to eat Avery? How would they get to her in time? They had figured all of The Otherwoods was monster territory. How much worse were The Centertrees?

"Maybe that's not the right word . . ." Xavier tapped his chin. "Bait? Since it seems to be you they're after."

River suppressed frustrated tears. They felt incredibly unlucky. Even knowing that they couldn't be possessed by a spirit with Pancakes at their side, they weren't sure they could fight monsters. There was so much they didn't know about The Otherwoods—they felt silly for thinking clean underwear would be the worst of their worries. River needed someone who could help them navigate this world.

They needed an actual hero. Someone who didn't freeze up in front of monsters and knew The Otherwoods well.

Someone who was good at saving people. Like Xavier.

"Can you help me?"

Xavier blinked. "Why would I help you?"

Good question. "Because, well, you're already dead? What do you have to lose?"

"Wow," Xavier said, drawing out the syllable. River felt a little bad. Maybe that was considered rude too? They didn't really know spirit etiquette. "A fair point, but a low blow. Say I do help you, what's in it for me?"

River didn't know; they didn't really have much to offer. "Um . . . is there anything you'd want from me?"

Xavier thought for a long moment. Finally, his expression lit up. "I got it! After I help you save your friend, you have to let me possess you long enough to get some ice cream. I've been in The Otherwoods for a while now, I should have the power to do it." His face grew serious. "At least two scoops, and you're paying for it."

River blinked. "That's all?"

The spirit's expression was grave. "You have no idea how much I miss ice cream, River. No. Idea." He stuck out his hand. "Do we have a deal?"

River thought they should probably get more details on the nature of possession, but they were desperate. Besides, they would die without Xavier. A quick possession was an easy trade compared with failing alone. They shook Xavier's hand.

"Awesome," Xavier said. "Besides, I have nothing to do anyway, so I probably would've agreed regardless. Do me a favor and leave any bargaining to me."

River was fine with that but hoped they wouldn't come to regret the decision to spend a lot of time with Xavier.

"So, where do we go from here?" River asked.

"Well, it's a bit of a walk to get to The Centertrees," Xavier started. "But before we can think of that, we need to prepare. Get you cleaned up and ready for a rescue mission."

"How do we do that?" River asked.

Xavier smiled. "We go where all the spirits who unfortunately ended up in The Otherwoods go: The City of Souls."

13

The City of Souls

After seeing nothing but the same somber trees for ages, River was both shocked and relieved to learn that they were quite close to The City of Souls. Even though they were a little nervous because that sounded like the kind of place they'd happily avoid. It was never The City of Puppies and Kittens or The City of Chocolate Chip Cookies. No, it *had* to be ghosts. It seemed that there was a lot more to The Otherwoods than River initially thought.

It wasn't a nice surprise. There was something more sinister about organized evil. After all, Ms. Deery's classroom was practically spotless.

They walked about ten minutes more before River got their first glimpse of the city. The trees faded out, and there it was. A skyline of jagged, colorful, shining buildings. Even bigger than what River was used to. It almost looked like they'd momentarily stepped out of The Otherwoods. The buildings shimmered with lights—the closest thing to stars in The Otherwoods so far.

"There you are," Xavier said. "The City of Souls. Just a little farther."

River stopped to admire the twinkling city from that distance, but they needed to keep on schedule. With Pancakes next to them, they started back after Xavier.

"What did you mean earlier by 'the spirits who unfortunately ended up in The Otherwoods'?" River asked. "Not everyone who dies comes here?"

"Of course not. The Otherwoods is where the monsters and never-quite-alive beings come from. All that dark stuff." Xavier had a habit of answering everything matter-of-factly, which was nice, but also a bit condescendingly, which wasn't. "The Elsewhere is the spirit realm for all that was living, like humans. But sometimes, some of us accidentally end up here instead."

That was a big accident.

"How?" River asked. "Or . . . why?"

Xavier paused a moment, foot nearly freezing in the air before he resumed movement and set it down on a lone crunchy gray leaf. The trees faded around them, and only a flat field of short, dead grass remained between River and Xavier and the city. "There's some running theories, but we can't say for sure."

"What are the theories?" River asked.

Xavier shrugged. "Doesn't matter right now. Let's focus on getting to The City of Souls, huh?"

The spirit's tone was light, but there was something off in his eyes. Sad, almost. Maybe the conversation was tough for Xavier. River couldn't imagine that anyone would choose to come to The Otherwoods over The Elsewhere. Sure, they didn't know what The Elsewhere was like, but if it didn't have monsters? Clearly the better option.

"Okay, what's The City of Souls, then?" River asked. Their eyes darted down to Pancakes, who was doing a good job of keeping pace. "Like, how did that happen *here*?" River gestured to the grandeur of the city ahead of them.

"Over time, enough spirits gathered and stayed together. As more and more came, they created a city to remind them of the human world, and maybe feel a little better about being stuck here instead." Xavier shrugged again. "Plus, the monsters stay away."

River didn't know how to feel about a city that looked something like home in this other, darker world. On one hand, it would be a nice reprieve from the endless trees. On the other . . .

They bit back thoughts about their mom and dad, who probably were worried sick looking for them right now. But it would all be okay once River returned with Avery. They just had to find her. That was more important than missing their parents.

At the very least, they were extremely glad the monsters stayed away from where they were headed.

"What about the spirits I see in the human world? Why aren't they in a spirit realm?"

"Portals work both ways, River. If we come across them, we can go through them too. But only to the human world; there aren't really portals to The Elsewhere. Some spirits like to visit places from their old life—I mean, can you blame them if this is their only other option?" Xavier gestured widely to The Otherwoods surrounding them.

"Have you ever gone back?"

"A couple times. We can't stay for long, though; it uses too much energy. But I don't like doing it anyway. It got kinda depressing, especially after my memory started to go. I knew there were people I was looking for, but I couldn't remember who they were," he explained sadly.

Another thing for River to feel bad about asking. They changed the subject. "Do monsters attack spirits?"

"Not really," Xavier said.

"What do monsters eat, then?"

Xavier sighed, before looking right into River's eyes. "Little kids who ask too many questions."

"Rude." River rolled their eyes. "And I'm not a little kid."

Pancakes meowed, probably in agreement. River decided to take it that way.

At that point, they were right up to the city, and the dull gold grass had morphed into concrete. Buildings coated the land, with architecture styles from across the globe. There weren't any cars, but sidewalks connected buildings over the ground, dirt and grass peeking from the spaces between. Tons of colored lights illuminated the buildings.

The only thing that gave River a strange feeling was the variety of plants and flowers around the city. Like the grass, all of them were dead, wilted, and grayed. Not a single natural green could be found, despite the neon lights decorating the brick and stone.

"Come on," Xavier said. "We can rest when we get there."

River wasn't sure if they had much time for rest, not when they didn't know what Avery was going through. They wanted to find her and get out of The Otherwoods as quickly as possible. But they also figured they wouldn't have much of a choice. Running from two different monsters in the same day, hiking through the seemingly endless woods, and falling twice had taken a toll on their body. Lying down for a moment sounded like a dream.

But dreams were too good to be true, and the city almost felt the same way.

Should they really trust the spirits here? Xavier had agreed to help and saved River, but that didn't mean he was right about taking the detour. The Otherwoods had wanted River for so long, and there were those threats they'd received even before entering.

Now that River was here, what would The Otherwoods do?

And would The City of Souls really be safe in the meantime?

The buildings grew taller and brighter as they moved deeper into the city, and River got a better look at the bustling crowds. There were certainly plenty of spirits that looked like normal humans, but there were just as many that didn't. They were blends of animals, or mostly faceless, or with ghostly appearances River never could've thought up.

Xavier must've noticed the expression on River's face, because he leaned in to whisper, "Not all spirits were human once, you know."

River had seen a few inhuman or almost-but-not-quite human spirits before, but it wasn't something they could get used to easily, and they tried not to stare.

As many looks as River was receiving for being human and shockingly not dead, Pancakes was getting even more attention. Some spirits gave the cat a little nod or bow in respect as he trotted along next to River.

As they strolled by, River could make out some of the whispers from the spirits around them, at least the ones that were in English.

"A little young, don't you think . . ."

"Just in time, though."

"Too bad a cat's got them, otherwise someone could go and possess the kid . . ."

River didn't know what they were talking about, but they were certainly glad they had Pancakes with them. And Xavier seemed to be glaring at all the spirits who spoke around them, so maybe he was a good ally to have too.

The whole situation was overwhelming. All of River's senses were sharpened, but they still felt a strange sense of awe. The colored lights were beautiful, but so bright that the individual bulbs flared out like falling comets. As River and Xavier continued through the crowd, human spirits continued to speak a variety of different languages to each other, all the words blending and amplifying in River's ears. They weren't sure if they wanted to run away from the city or deeper into it.

"You okay?" Xavier asked.

River shrugged. "A little overwhelmed."

River wasn't sure what they'd expected The Other-woods to be like, but they hadn't been prepared for it to be so big. It included an entire city just for spirits. They didn't know how expansive the monster territory was. How would River find Avery in all of that?

Xavier gave a friendly slap on their back. "You'll be fine, kid. Don't pay attention to any of them. Let me get a place for us to stay the night. We'll head out first thing in the morning. For now, go look around. Have some fun."

River's heart jumped in their chest. "Alone?"

"You'll be safe with Pancakes. Like I said, ignore the others."

River looked down at Pancakes, who didn't seem sure about the plan either. River looked back at Xavier. "How will you find me?"

Xavier brushed off their concern. "I'm excellent at finding people."

He disappeared into the crowd, and a large spirit with a long snout and a business suit blocked River from following him.

It had hardly been twenty minutes and Xavier was proving to be an irresponsible partner. Just when River thought he was trustworthy, he left them alone.

Sure, Xavier probably had a good reason. It didn't make River less bitter about the fact.

River remained where they stood. They weren't sure which direction to go look around in, because everywhere they turned, spirits still shot them looks, the murmurs now too quiet to hear but loud as they piled on top of each other. Some spirits seemed to look at River with excitement, some with pity, and some with an unsettling expression that River could only think of as hunger.

River picked up Pancakes for some extra protection. He was probably tired from all the walking, and didn't seem to mind.

"Well, hopefully, we weren't abandoned completely," River muttered to Pancakes. Even though that was exactly how they felt. Pancakes didn't appear to care either way. He closed his eyes and started purring. Maybe he was happy to be held, or maybe he'd found Xavier rather annoying.

To be fair, Pancakes tended to find everyone annoying.

Armed with their cat that supposedly offered possession protection, River continued to walk through the city. Because they already drew enough attention by being human, they tried not to be accidentally rude and stare at the spirits with a wide variety of appearances. All River's experience in not meeting the eyes of or giving attention to otherworldly beings proved useful among these spirits that couldn't seem to look away from them. Luckily, the city itself provided enough distraction.

Although all the dead flowers in the shop windows were a little unnerving, the bright lights and vibrant paint colors lightened the mood. There were bookstores, clothing stores, a shocking number of food stalls that smelled delicious (though there was a notable lack of ice cream), and a range of different businesses and what appeared to be apartments.

River was really tempted to stop for a steamed bun, but they weren't sure what kind of money was used in The Otherwoods, and whatever it was, they were pretty sure they didn't have it. Maybe when Xavier came back.

If Xavier came back.

River had to hold out hope—the spirit did really seem to want that ice cream.

Plus, the idea of casually eating street food while Avery was out there with monsters didn't feel right at all. Was she really at that place Xavier said—The Centertrees? Did she have any food?

Panic rose, and they held Pancakes a little bit tighter.

Please wait for me . . . We're here now, River thought, like she would somehow be able to hear it.

Avery had to be okay. River didn't have a chance of finding her before, but they did now. It wasn't just them, alone. They had Xavier.

Well, they *mostly* had Xavier.

They had to hope it would all be enough.

Their skin crawled with the feeling of being watched.

Despite the attention from the other spirits, none of them made a move toward River. It was probably Pancakes' protection. Whatever the reason, River was thankful. They focused on the feeling of Pancakes' breathing and soft fur to keep them from getting too lost in their head, senses, and worries.

River stopped in front of a building painted olive green. It had two store windows on either side of the door, but both were covered in smooth purple fabrics. The door was ornate, with small golden spirals, and was also purple, in a shade so dark it mirrored the night sky.

River's eyes drifted up to the printing above the door. PSYCHIC

They had never been to a psychic before, although they did think one in a spirit realm probably had more credibility than any back home. Would that person be able to tell them more about where Avery was? Sure, Xavier had an idea, but it couldn't hurt to get confirmation, or maybe even some specifics.

They had no idea how services in The City of Souls worked. What if they charged something worse than a currency River didn't have, like vials of blood or River's right eyeball?

They happened to like their right eyeball exactly where it was in their head.

Still, the psychic might know something that would help them get to Avery faster.

River opened the door and stepped inside.

14

The Sarcastic Psychic

The inside of the building was dim, lit only by candles of various shapes and colors. There were also a lot of books, which felt like a fire hazard, but River tended to notice that kind of stuff more after the mishap with Charles's slime. Overstuffed shelves lined the walls, but the room was nearly empty in the middle. The back wall, directly across from the door, had a curtain, and in front of the curtain was a counter with a little bell on it.

White smoke filled the air, swirling in the bit of light that poured through a window in the ceiling. It acted as a kind of spotlight, pointing directly at the bell. River figured they were supposed to ring it.

As the door softly closed behind them, Pancakes jumped

out of their arms, then started sniffing the floors and walls. It might've been a good sign that he didn't seem afraid, but Pancakes was also a fearless cat.

Instead of walking directly to the bell, River stepped toward a shelf. In addition to the books and candles, there was an assortment of random objects. River stopped in front of a few jars, coated in dust. They rubbed some dust off one, and saw a chunk of monster flesh floating in liquid.

River jumped back, causing Pancakes' fur to rise.

Maybe looking around wasn't such a good idea. Maybe coming inside hadn't been a good idea in the first place.

River walked toward the curtain at the back of the room. It was the same purple fabric that blocked out the windows. There was nothing on the small counter in front of it aside from the small golden bell.

They hit the top to ring it.

Almost immediately, as if their presence was expected, the curtain shot open. River screamed at the sudden sight of the woman in front of them, but she only smiled. While almost certainly a spirit, she seemed very human. She was an adult, but not as old as River's parents, and had long red nails that were pointed like claws. Her eyes were a dark blue, but the lids were shaded bright yellow. As she smiled, River saw that she had an extra set of canine teeth.

It was an almost scary appearance, but compared with what River had already seen in The Otherwoods, it could hardly be considered as such.

"Welcome," the psychic said. "I see you are interested in a reading. What's your name?"

River waved away the smoke to see better. "I'm surprised you don't already know."

They thought a bit of humor might help everything feel less creepy.

"Well, I was trying to be polite, River Rydell. But I suppose we can just skip the pleasantries, then, huh?"

They were wrong.

A shiver ran up River's spine, and they immediately wished they had replied normally. It was much worse to have a stranger know their identity. "How . . . how'd you know that?"

The psychic laughed. "Now you're surprised? I have more power here than I did on Earth, sensing someone's name is easy." She tapped her long nails against the surface of the counter, one falling right after the other. "And of course I know who you are. Everyone's been waiting for your arrival. Even without having seen you before, I could smell the magic from a mile away."

Magic? It wasn't like River had any magical powers, unless seeing ghosts and monsters counted, and that certainly didn't feel like magic. Whatever it was that made River different, the psychic was able to sense it.

River could only assume that was a very bad thing. And why was everyone waiting for them? Was it the arrival of River that mattered, or were they looking for anyone to cross over and River just happened to be an easier target? It didn't matter much; they were very uncomfortable either way.

"What's your name?" River asked, because they weren't

sure they wanted answers on that yet. "Since you already know mine."

"Natalia," the psychic said. "Pleasure to meet you. So, the reading?"

River shifted from one foot to the other. They didn't know if it was the smoke or the fire from all the candles, but the room felt far too warm. "I don't have any money."

Xavier may have been right in saying they should avoid bargaining.

Natalia hit all four nails against the counter and leaned her cheek on her other hand. "Who says I'm asking for money?"

River gulped. That was it. She'd ask for blood, or River's right eyeball. Maybe even a kidney. River was pretty sure they only needed one, but they certainly didn't want to give either of them up if they didn't have to.

"What are you asking for?"

Natalia leaned forward across the counter, so close River could see the navy flecks in her eyes. "Your soul."

River's breath caught, fear pouring out of them along with the words. This psychic probably wasn't a spirit, but a demon. "No, sorry, not for sale. I don't know what you'd do with it, but I need it for when I'm probably killed here."

A tense moment passed, with River ready to grab their cat and head back toward the door.

Then Natalia burst out laughing, slapping her hand against the counter.

"You should have seen your face, kid. Priceless." She

wiped away a tear. "And nice confidence, my stars. No, I can't take your soul. And money doesn't exist here. It's a level playing field when you're dead. Readings are on the house."

River was both relieved and embarrassed. Did all spirits have such an annoying sense of humor? They took a deep breath. "I need to know where my friend Avery Davis is. She was taken here by a monster."

"All right." Natalia lifted her hands in the air, as if gathering energy. She closed her eyes as she sucked in a breath, then slowly lowered her arms as she opened her eyes and looked right at River. "Leave."

River blinked. Was that the whole reading? She hadn't even read anything, and that wasn't an answer to their question. River figured there would be tarot cards, or a crystal ball, or at least a glance at their palm. At the very minimum, a suggestion about where to look for Avery.

"What?" River asked. "That doesn't help me, I need to know where she is."

Natalia raised an eyebrow. "Oh, I'm sorry, was I not clear?" She gestured to the door. "Forget about your friend. Leave this shop and go back through whatever portal you slipped through. You don't want to be in The Otherwoods. Get out. Go. Run for your life and pretend none of this happened."

River's stomach started to hurt again. "I can't leave her. It's my fault Avery's here in the first place; we have to save her." Pancakes brushed against their legs in likely agreement.

The psychic was silent for a moment. A loud kind of silence that filled the room.

"Well, that's really up to you," she said finally. "But if you do stay, I wouldn't keep making those jokes about dying. It's not funny when it's doomed to come true."

River's chest tightened and iced over. Was she serious? If River stayed in The Otherwoods, they wouldn't make it out alive? What would happen to them then? Would they be stuck as a spirit here forever?

"Then tell me what you know," River said. They tried to stand a little straighter. "Even if I am doomed, I have to know how to save her."

For the first time since River had arrived, the psychic's face showed emotion. There was sadness in her eyes when she next spoke. "Would you really be willing to give up everything?"

River didn't know what she meant by that, but they wanted information.

"Yeah," they said. "I am."

Natalia didn't meet River's eyes. "Maybe you shouldn't be."

Before River could question her, the shop door flew open. Both River and Pancakes twisted to see Xavier at the door.

"Back on your theatrics, Natalia?" Xavier gave as a cold greeting. "I've heard rumors."

The psychic resumed the tapping of her fingernails against the counter. She didn't seem to pay the other spirit any mind. "Making friends already, River? A good one, I hope. You might need them."

There was something sad and far away in her voice. River wanted to say something, but Xavier turned to them first. "Told you I'd find you. Now, let's go."

Uncertain, River picked up Pancakes and met Xavier at the door. They could feel Natalia's eyes on them, but she didn't say anything more. Xavier looked annoyed. "Don't worry about whatever she said," he muttered. "She's always talking about doom and gloom to everyone. Better to just ignore it. Some people miss the drama of living a little too much."

That should've made River feel a lot better, but it didn't. Even if it was something the psychic did often, it felt real. Like there was some truth expressed in her words. Maybe it was just River's worry talking. But it was hard not to be worried when someone insisted you'd die soon.

"Right," River said.

They looked back, hoping to get something from Natalia's expression, but the psychic was gone, purple curtain shut as if it had never been disturbed.

15

The Inn of Spirits

The place Xavier found for them to rest was better than River anticipated. Apparently, wayward spirits really had a high bar for hotel and inn accommodations in The Otherwoods. Still following the theme of bright lights and colors, the inn had hot baths and an infinity pool, plush beds in spacious rooms, and a variety of artworks by a few successful artists who apparently had gotten trapped in The Otherwoods after death. It was the nicest place River had ever been to, and possibly the nicest place they'd ever go to, since money wasn't a factor.

Aside from the plants, River was shocked at how *alive* the city was. Unlike the rest of The Otherwoods, there was a sparkle in the air, a bustling energy, as well as the smell of baked bread and cinnamon.

Inside the inn, there weren't any of the dead floral arrangements.

"It's a bit too gloomy to be resting around flowers," Xavier had said in response to River's question about it. "Sure, we're dead, but we don't need to feel like corpses. Such a bummer."

And The Inn of Spirits was no bummer.

Of course, River didn't do much to enjoy it. Once they walked into their room, the need for sleep caught up with them, and they immediately passed out on the bed.

When they woke up the next morning, they felt much better—not necessarily well rested (Pancakes somehow took up half the bed), but still better.

Maybe "better" wasn't the right term. As they wiped the sleep from their eyes, the gravity of the situation fell on them again. It was hard to feel better about anything with Avery still lost and a very unhelpful psychic predicting their death.

"Morning, kid. I grabbed these for you while you were asleep," Xavier said, tossing them clothes to change into. "Get dressed and we can head out."

The promise of another day in The Otherwoods didn't exactly brighten River's spirits, but hopefully the sooner they left, the sooner they'd find Avery and get back home. Mustering up all the energy an almost good night's sleep provided, River got out of bed and headed to the bathroom.

After changing the bandage on their arm, they slid into the salmon-colored shorts, white T-shirt, and navy jacket. It was a small relief to change after their old outfit had been stained in dirt, sweat, and monster blood.

They could practically hear their mother groaning at the choice to wear a white shirt on a rescue mission that was sure to be messy. River's eyes stung at the thought of her.

Once again, more than anything, they wished their parents had believed them. Maybe then they would've been here with River. There wouldn't be any issue saving Avery, because they'd have found a way.

Instead, a teen ghost, a cat, and River were her only hope.

River didn't like the odds, if they were being honest.

They exited the bathroom to rejoin Xavier, who was packing and repacking as Pancakes licked himself on the bed.

"I'm surprised you have clothes here," River said.

Xavier rolled his eyes. "Just because we're dead doesn't mean we want to go walking around naked, River."

"I know, but I thought the clothes would just be . . . what you died in?" They hoped that didn't sound insensitive.

"I was hit by a car." Xavier gestured to his neat outfit. "I certainly didn't look like this. No, we can still wear clothes here. It all comes from the magic of being in a spirit realm, which is why we can touch and eat." Xavier flicked River on the forehead gently, his hand turning translucent. "You, however, are not from a spirit realm, which is why it still takes a lot of energy to touch you."

River nodded. That made sense, and at any rate, they were grateful for the clean clothes.

Xavier picked up a bag and smiled. "We should start heading out, but I thought we could stop for some breakfast first. This inn is particularly known for its waffle bar." He gave a thoughtful look at Pancakes. "And they have fish available all the time."

"I don't know." River shouldered their backpack and looked at Xavier. "We should be going after Avery." Their stomach grumbled loudly.

Xavier rolled his eyes. "I don't think you'll be much help to her if you're starved to death."

River didn't know how to argue with that. They just hoped she would be okay. "Can I eat the food here?"

"Of course," Xavier said. "You'll just never be able to return home."

River glared at them. "How can I take you for ice cream if I can't return home?"

"I'm only kidding, you can eat it, you'll be fine." He rolled his eyes again. "You're so serious, River. Have you ever laughed in your life?"

"What's laughter?" River asked. "Never heard of it."

"Well, sarcasm is a form of humor, so I'm taking it."

River didn't normally consider themself a very serious person. They cuddled their cat at night and walked like a T-rex when they were scared—those weren't very serious things. But they'd gone through a lot in the past two days: getting injured by a monster, losing their only friend to that same monster, sneaking into The Otherwoods and almost getting killed by *another* monster . . .

They'd dealt with enough monsters to make them a bit more serious than they'd be otherwise.

The spirits' sense of humor only made it more difficult to trust anything anyway.

Xavier led them down the stairs and past the lobby to where breakfast was served. Trotting along next to River, Pancakes stopped to take a drink from the large fountain, stepping right over the edge to lap up water from the base. No one said anything or tried to stop him. Most of the spirits seemed to like cats, despite the previous disappointment of being unable to possess River because of one.

The dining area was as cozy as the rest of the inn, with tables set up that had grayed daisies in the middle and dry leaves spread around. A faceless spirit somehow sipped coffee, but River tried not to be rude and stare to figure out how, and a human spirit sat next to a doglike spirit at another table nearby, sharing a plate of pastries. A few other various spirits cleaned up plates or chatted at tables.

River hardly noticed, because their attention had been entirely grabbed by the food.

It was set out in a buffet and was just about anything they could ask for. Eggs and sausage, rice and beans, cakes and cookies, meats and cheese, a few different types of fish. Their jaw dropped at the sight.

"If you have all this, why don't you have ice cream?" River asked Xavier.

His expression tightened with pain. "It's the one thing we can't get right." He shrugged. "Besides, even if we did have it, we can't taste anything as spirits. But the act of eating can remind us of home, and it all looks nice." Xavier's eyes narrowed. "You trying to back out of our deal?"

"No, jeez, I'm just asking." River crossed their arms over their rumbling stomach. "You help me get Avery back, and we'll get ice cream wherever you want. I promise."

That seemed to appease Xavier, who smiled and pulled River toward the buffet line. They piled on food for themself and made a plate with fish that looked safe for Pancakes. The three took a table, and Pancakes dug into his first fillet.

Since River wasn't a spirit, the food was delicious. Xavier didn't seem too impressed, but he ate anyway.

It was surprisingly nice, eating breakfast among the spirits, but River couldn't help but feel like it was a little *too* nice. The kind of nice that felt like an appetizer for impending doom. It made River want to leave faster. Not only because they really did need to get to Avery, but because while The City of Souls was comfortable, getting comfortable anywhere in The Otherwoods seemed like a bad idea.

"How far is it to The Centertrees?" River asked Xavier.

He took a bite of a cookie. "It's not really the distance that's the problem, it's the danger."

"Oh good," River said, the food in their stomach suddenly churning. "I was worried it'd be boring."

Maybe Xavier had been right about their sarcasm. If anything, River *hoped* it would be boring. They thrived on the boring. Things had been much too interesting for them lately, and it had been terrible.

"Nothing's boring when I'm around," Xavier said matter-of-factly.

River wasn't sure if it was a joke or if the spirit had that much confidence.

They set down their fork. They still had some food left on their plate, but they were already full, and with the trees as their only bathroom, they really didn't want to go overboard right before the journey. They had a limited amount of toilet paper with them, after all.

They did, for a moment, wonder if spirits pooped, but decided against asking because that was probably ruder than asking how they died.

"You done?" Xavier asked.

River nodded.

"You didn't try the waffle bar." He said it like it was an absolute sin.

"I know." River shrugged. "I don't exactly feel great about eating when my friend is in danger."

It was true. Guilt had been eating away at River like Pancakes ate away at the fish, licking the already cleaned bones. Xavier's expression softened in a manner that made him look way more human, but River didn't want to tell him that.

"Don't worry, you're doing what you have to do," Xavier said. "The fact that you're here says a lot. There aren't many people who would travel to a whole new world for their friend. Like I said, you have to be alive to get to her. So, go easy on yourself. You have a lot to be proud of."

River's chest did loosen a little at Xavier's words. It was a shockingly nice thing to say, and River needed to hear it.

"Besides," Xavier continued, "they'll keep her alive since it's you they're after. Don't worry about that. It's your life you should be worried about."

River's chest tightened right back up. While it was reassuring to know Avery would likely be okay, it didn't make them feel better with the near-death warning they'd already received.

They still didn't know *why* the monsters were after them.

"I really wish you'd stopped after the first part," River muttered.

Xavier winked. "You get the spirit guide you paid for."

Apparently, ice cream didn't get much in The City of Souls.

"I'll check us out from here." Xavier hopped up from the table and pointed toward the lobby. "Give me five minutes, and then meet me outside."

River nodded. They didn't know what the checkout process was, but since money wasn't really a thing in The Otherwoods, they couldn't feel too bad. Besides, if Xavier was going to temporarily possess them *and* leave them alone at random times, he'd have to pull his weight somehow.

River wrapped some leftover dry food in napkins and

stuck it in their backpack. As they put their backpack around their shoulders again, a piece of paper fluttered to the floor. River picked it up. They didn't recognize the handwriting, and the message itself wasn't that clear.

In The Otherwoods, your fear is their power, but their magic is yours.

They looked around, but no one was watching them with new interest or was close enough to have slipped the note inside.

When could someone have put it in their backpack? Only Xavier had been with them in the room, and he didn't seem like the type to leave notes. Unless Pancakes had suddenly learned how to write, that left few options.

What did it mean? *Your fear is their power*? That sure made whoever it was pretty powerful, because River was feeling especially frightened now.

Maybe it was a prank? After all, between Xavier and the psychic, spirits seemed to have a weird sense of humor.

They crumpled up the note but stuck it in the pocket of their shorts. River didn't feel like being alone anymore, so they scooped up Pancakes and walked outside the inn, where Xavier was already waiting.

River pulled out the note and showed it to Xavier. "Did you leave this for me?" River asked. "It was in my bag."

Xavier took a minute to read the note and frowned. "I have no idea what this means. Probably a spirit messing with you. Some of them are jealous you're of the living, so I wouldn't worry about it. Let me know if anything like this happens again, and I'll protect you, okay?"

He crumpled the slip of paper and tossed it on the ground. Still, River's stomach sank with worry. But they told themself it was mostly worry over everything else. Xavier had to be right. Clearly spirits did enjoy messing around. If Xavier wasn't worried about the strange message, River shouldn't be either.

Besides, with Xavier promising to protect them, the other worries didn't seem all that bad. "Okay."

"Ready?" Xavier asked.

River gave him a look. "Does it matter if I am or not?"

"Not really." He patted River on the shoulder. "Time to save your girl from some monsters."

16

The Rescue Mission Begins

With what had seemed like either ten minutes or two hours of walking, The City of Souls was already lost to the fog, and River, Xavier, and Pancakes were back in the trees. Once again among the same bent branches overhead that kept reaching in and the endless dark trunks that sprouted from the dirt, River lost all sense of time. The city had been a short break from the monotony, but back in the forest, they fell right into that endless loop.

When Pancakes didn't feel like walking, he slept in River's or Xavier's arms. Pancakes still didn't seem to particularly like Xavier, but he knew a free pillow when he saw one.

River's body was tense. They anticipated a monster at every corner and started thinking of all the opportunities one had to appear. From behind any of the trees, hidden in the thick fog, flying down from the sky, or perhaps even bursting up from the dirt. It felt like nowhere was safe.

It was a feeling, River supposed, they would have to get used to.

"Why is it that you can see us?" Xavier asked out of the blue. "Spirits and monsters, I mean."

Xavier's question temporarily distracted River from the never-ending sense of danger. "I don't know," River said. "It's always been that way. I was hoping you'd know."

"Hmmm," Xavier said, drawing out the syllable. "Just makes me wonder, you know. Why you?"

River wondered that same thing nearly every day, usually with a lot of self-pity and more recently with words they wouldn't say in front of their parents.

They sighed. "I don't know. If I had any choice, I would've given it to someone else." They paused, wondering if that was actually true. They certainly didn't want this ability themself, but would they be able to curse someone else with it? Maybe a bad person. Or someone braver who could handle this kind of stuff. Rather than think too much about it, they slightly changed the conversation's direction. "I guess it's like my gender. It's just the way I was made. I don't know why or how, only that it's who I am."

Xavier scratched Pancakes behind the ears. "That makes sense. I wouldn't know what to say if someone asked how I knew I was a boy." He looked at River. "You know, I kissed a boy once. When I was alive."

That got River's attention. They practically stopped in

their tracks. It's not like River was able to talk to other queer people in person often; they didn't talk to anyone in person often. "Really?"

Xavier nodded eagerly, then jutted his lip. "Well, we were sort of pushed into each other. So it was more of an accident, and my mouth bled after."

"I don't think that's the same thing," River said gently.

"Fair enough, but I think it's cool." Xavier grinned smugly at River. "I'm sure you never kissed anyone, since you're an elementary schooler."

"I'm a *middle* schooler, first of all." River rolled their eyes.

Sure, River never had kissed anyone, but they didn't need Xavier to talk to them like a child because of it. They'd probably kiss someone, maybe even multiple someones, by the time they were as old as Xavier.

"Do you like this friend of yours?" Xavier asked. "Avery, right?"

Despite the direction this conversation had taken, River did not expect that question. They couldn't stop their face from heating up. "No," they muttered.

Xavier put on his most annoying smile, and River was pretty sure he had plenty. "You *do* like her." River stared forward at the endless trees, refusing to look Xavier's way. Apparently, that was enough for him to confirm his suspicions. "No wonder you're doing all this for her."

River's face was far too hot at this point. They didn't like how easily Xavier could embarrass them. "She's my *friend*."

"Yeah, I had a friend like that. I was crushing so hard."

Xavier shook his head. "You don't have to be so embarrassed about it. It's better to just tell them."

"It's not that easy," River protested.

"It's not." Xavier bit his lip. "But it's way harder when you realize you lost your chance."

Xavier looked younger in that moment, honest and vulnerable. Gone were his usual sarcasm and smirk. Xavier was being real with River—really real—for the first time since they'd met, and it meant a lot to them. River thought of all the things they still had to look forward to that Xavier wouldn't have the chance to do. Dying young seemed cruel enough, and now here he was, stuck in the wrong, nightmarish afterlife.

River's voice was soft. "Is that why you're . . . here?"

"Maybe. Could be part of the reason. From what I heard, spirits that have regrets, or a strong enough hold on the world of the living, can't pass on until those are gone. So we end up in a spirit realm."

"So this isn't . . . *the end* the end?" River asked.

Xavier shook his head. "Supposedly not. And I've seen enough spirits actually pass on—bright light, look of calmness, all that jazz—to believe it."

"Wow." It was a lot to take in, but River couldn't help but feel a tiny bit relieved that if something *did* go very wrong, they likely wouldn't be stuck in The Otherwoods for all eternity.

Xavier continued. "Usually spirits that don't pass on right away end up in The Elsewhere, a limbo for the once-living, like I said earlier. I was just lucky enough to end up in The Otherwoods instead."

"It doesn't make sense, though," River said, shaking their head. "Why?"

Xavier laughed. "I'm starting to think maybe there was just something wrong with me."

His jaw tightened, and his cheeks sank in like he was biting them. River nodded.

"Honestly? I feel that way a lot too."

Neither of them could talk for a moment, but it was a comfortable silence. Pancakes shifted in Xavier's arms.

"So none of the spirits have any idea why you all ended up here instead?"

With a sigh, Xavier looked at River. "The most popular theory is that the spirits here were closer to the spirit realms when they were alive. So while most of us couldn't see monsters and spirits like you, there was some small connection that brought us here anyway."

River swallowed. "Then I would have ended up here someday even if I hadn't come now?"

Xavier nodded. "Probably, yeah."

River didn't exactly feel happy to know they were destined to cross paths with The Otherwoods, but at least there would be a way out then. And while they weren't excited about it, they weren't exactly surprised either.

"I'm gonna pass on eventually." Xavier had an expression on his face that was unreadable. Something almost wistful, like a pleasant memory.

"Why can't you pass on now?" River asked. "What's holding you back?"

"Are you my new friend or my therapist?" Xavier shoved

them a little with his shoulder. "You're not the only one who's running after someone, kid."

River didn't know what that meant, but Xavier didn't seem like he wanted to explain. At least, not at that time. Still, he'd called River his friend. They couldn't help but smile a little at that.

River looked ahead at the trees, and the shadowy outline of more trees up ahead, and the break between them—

The break between them?

"What's that?" River asked. There hadn't been such a wide space between any of the trees since they'd walked into The Otherwoods forest.

Xavier bit his lip, which River had already learned was not a sign of good news. "That's The Cursed Bridge."

River tilted their head back and groaned. "And let me guess, there's no way to get where we're going without crossing it."

"Sorry, kid," Xavier said. "I told you it was dangerous."

They kept walking forward, and River could make out more of the scene. It was a pretty wide bridge, made completely of stone, with two large statues on either side of the entrance. It was still too far to see what they were.

"Well . . ." River kicked a rock out of the way. "What's the curse? Is it bad?"

Xavier made a face. "It depends . . . How easily do you get scared?"

Just like that, River had their answer.

It was going to be *really* bad.

17

The Cursed Bridge

River and Xavier stepped in front of the stone bridge. They were close enough now to clearly see the two giant statues on either end. Both had human bodies, but the one to the left had a crow's head and held a sword, and the one on the right had a lion's head and held an axe. River didn't know what either of them meant, but the design was cool.

Maybe a little unnerving, but cool nonetheless.

The bridge itself was about three feet wide and didn't have any railings past the statues. The three of them were at a complete cliff. River could see the land and trees on the other side, at least in shadows, but when they looked down . . . it was only a deadly drop into fog.

At least the stone pattern of the bridge looked sturdy, even if it was still terrifying.

"What, exactly, is the curse?" River asked, their voice a little higher than usual.

Xavier looked across the bridge with his lips tucked, an expression that both was silly and looked something like acceptance. "It has a strange way of using your fears against you to make you want to turn back."

"I already want to turn back," River admitted.

"Then you should be fine." He put a hand on River's shoulder, which was reassuring, though the hand started to disappear. "Just remember why you need to keep moving forward."

Pancakes, who had already jumped from Xavier's arms to make the world his litter box, trotted up to River and rubbed against their legs. At least River would have *him*. That way it wouldn't be so different from all the nights spent fearing Charles. It couldn't be worse than that, right?

At least, River hoped not.

"It'll be great," Xavier said, only to momentarily frown. "Well, no, it will probably be awful, but *you'll* be great." River looked helplessly at him, but he moved right along. "Promise."

Xavier stepped onto the bridge.

River had no choice but to follow.

"Ready?" River asked Pancakes. Pancakes gave a little mew in response.

River took a deep breath, and the duo stepped onto the bridge together.

Xavier was no longer in front of them. In fact, nothing was, aside from the path of the bridge. It felt a lot longer than it had looked, stretching out into the darkness. River peered over the edge, but it was only more of that endless black night.

"Xavier?"

No one answered. Even Pancakes, still at River's side, looked about as confused as a cat could look.

"Okay . . . ," River said, talking aloud more for their own sake. "I guess we keep walking forward?"

There didn't seem to be another option. If there had been a less brave option, River would've certainly taken it, but there was just endless bridge behind them where the ledge should have been. They figured they'd have better luck at least trying to move forward. So River started walking, and Pancakes followed.

Then River's foot sank into one of the stones, and the world around them shifted. In the panic, River picked up Pancakes. Instead of The Otherwoods forest, or the endless black air, they were suddenly standing in their history classroom.

But Pancakes was still in their arms, and the stone bridge was still underneath their feet. It went on past the classroom. They were still in The Otherwoods—they were being tricked.

Dread settled in River's stomach.

"What are you doing?" a voice snapped from behind them. "Do you really think *you* can be a hero?"

The voice was familiar. Not from The Otherwoods, but just as bone chilling.

When they turned around to face the classroom door, Ms. Deery stood there, blocking the path behind them. While she could normally be considered a fright any day, this Otherwoods version of her seemed exceptionally so. Her skin sagged, her eyes had a reddish tint, and she loomed taller than River remembered.

"Give up now," she taunted in her shrill voice. "You're a scared little kid with no friends. Avery doesn't like you. No one does." She cackled. Stretching out her fingers like claws, she leaned in over River. "You don't know who you are. Not a girl, not a boy, *certainly* not a hero." Her sinister smile was smug. "But I know who you are."

With her face filling most of River's vision, she called them a name that wasn't theirs.

The name that never belonged to them in the first place.

Tears sprang to River's eyes, and the words stabbed at their heart. Their deadname echoed all around them, repeating over and over and over again, seemingly getting louder each time. River closed their eyes and dug their face into Pancakes as if that would shut out the sound.

Seeing that her hate was effective, Ms. Deery gave a screeching laugh. "What a pathetic excuse for a hero. Avery deserves so much better than you. You can't even stand up to an old woman, let alone the hundreds of monsters who await you."

River sank to the ground, tears soaking Pancakes' fur. Ms. Deery was right—Avery did deserve better. What were they thinking, going after her? How could River have believed they were her only hope, when they were so . . .

hopeless? This classroom and Ms. Deery may have been fake, but everything she was saying felt like an undeniable truth.

Ms. Deery grew larger in size, shadow looming over River. The back of their eyelids went completely black but they couldn't shut out her loud voice. "Best do what I say and give up now, River."

Except she didn't say "River." She *never* said "River." Each time she said that name, it reverberated in their ears like a punch to the head. River tried to drown out the hurtful echo with their own thoughts: *That's not my name, that's not my name, that's not my name, that's not—*

It wasn't their name.

River's eyes popped open.

It wasn't their name.

Suddenly the things Ms. Deery was saying didn't feel like truth at all. She might as well have been speaking about someone else entirely. Someone who River never was and never would be.

They lifted their head from Pancakes' fur, looked up at Ms. Deery, and did the one thing they'd never been able to do in the real world.

"My name is River," they said.

Ms. Deery let out another screech, throwing her head back. As she tilted her head, the skin on either side ripped apart, revealing a monstrous face that was part demon but strangely birdlike. The bloody human skin flopped to the floor in front of River, as the red feathered smile laughed underneath.

River did what any reasonable person would have done at the sight.

They screamed.

Well, you can't win them all.

"River!"

River turned at the sound of Xavier's voice, relief washing over them. They ran toward him and away from the teacher. Xavier looked pained, beads of sweat forming on his face.

"How do we get out of the classroom?" River asked quickly.

"It's not a classroom for me," Xavier said. "It's different for everyone." Before River could ask what he was seeing, Xavier pulled on their arm. "Come on, we have to keep going."

They walked in the opposite direction they had come from.

Almost immediately, the scene around them changed. Pancakes growled in River's arms as the room around the bridge became their bedroom. For a moment, River again felt relieved. They had been homesick, and the illusion of their room was a welcome sight. The Pokémon poster in its proper place, their books and comics all lined up as they should be. But the bridge floor was still under their feet, so River knew better than to believe it.

The ground rumbled, the entire room seeming to shake.

"Do you feel that?" River asked Xavier.

"I don't feel anything," he responded, voice high and tight.

From under the bed, a giant bladed arm shot out and grabbed River's ankle. They screamed again and kicked it off, but a red cut opened on their skin. The limb dug into the floor past the stone bridge and pulled itself out from under the bed.

Charles was large enough, but this Cursed Bridge Charles was *huge*.

"What's happening to you?" Xavier called out. River clutched his arm and pulled Pancakes closer. Xavier's eyes looked glassy. "Are you bleeding?"

River couldn't answer, too distracted by the sight in front of them.

The bug creature had to bend over to fit in the room, and took up most of the space. It leaned directly over River and Xavier, opening its pincers wide and roaring, slime spraying everywhere.

Xavier couldn't see it. River didn't know what Xavier was seeing, but it had to be as terrifying as Charles from the way he shook.

It's not really Charles, it's not really real, River repeated in their head.

Their eyes were still filled with tears, but the thought gave them hope. That couldn't be Charles, because as terrifying as Charles was, he'd never tried to hurt River. And whether he meant to or not, he was the one that suggested River bring Pancakes along, which had saved River from death by monster *and* possession.

River felt the hopeless knot in their chest unravel.

Remembering the swell of confidence they'd felt standing up to Ms. Deery (before the whole face-splitting-open thing anyway), they faced fake Charles. "You're not Charles,"

River said. Then, to kick the illusion while it was down, they added, "And, honestly, your impression of Charles is terrible."

Pancakes hissed at the imposter for good measure.

"Who's Charles?" Xavier asked, but the question went unanswered.

Almost immediately, the setting changed. It dropped over River, Xavier, and Pancakes like the way night falls when you're distracted.

Any confidence River had gained sucked right out of them. They were in Avery's backyard. The stone path continued into the trees, but they could make out two tall statues. It had to be the end of the bridge. The other side.

It was still, quiet. All they could hear was the rapid beating of their own heart.

And then a scream.

River spun around to see Avery, on the ground with the monster standing right over her. It roared in her face, and tears rolled down her cheeks. River took a step forward, but then stopped themself.

It wasn't real.

Right?

The Avery in front of them screamed again, and then looked over at River. Her eyes widened with desperation.

"River," she called. "Please! Help me!"

River shot forward, but Xavier grabbed them. "River, what are you doing? That's the wrong way!"

River shook their head, trying to break from Xavier's grasp. "No, it's Avery, I have to save her. I can't lose her again." They blinked, wishing the sight would change. "It's my fault, it's my fault."

Xavier turned River and forced them to look into his eyes. "That's not her, River. That's not the real Avery. If you want to save her, keep moving forward with me, okay?"

River felt a few tears fall. They had to go back. "I can't, I came here to save her, I need to—"

"You need to keep moving." Xavier's tone was strong and sure. "That's not real, it's all the bridge. I promise. We're what's real." His voice cracked, tears pooling in his eyes. "We're real. Okay? We're real. Only us."

With the fear in his voice, it felt like Xavier was saying it more for himself than for River. Whatever the bridge used to haunt Xavier must have been equally terrifying, and as much as it hurt, River knew the brave spirit was right.

"River," Avery's voice cried. "Please."

It tore at River's heart. They were afraid of the scene in front of them, of everything in The Otherwoods. They were afraid Ms. Deery and her deadnaming were right and they'd mess everything up because they didn't like who they were, if they actually knew who that person was in the first place.

But the real Avery was in danger, and they'd promised they'd save her. She was the only person who saw them, who believed them. Maybe with her, they'd be able to see themself in the same way.

Holding on tightly to Pancakes, River nodded at Xavier.

Trying desperately to ignore the screams, they all ran to the end of the bridge.

18

The Boy Afraid of Nothing

Once their foot hit the ground on the other side of the bridge, everything snapped back to normal. They were in The Otherwoods, with the dirt path below them and the hideous trees they'd never been so excited to see.

River looked back. The Cursed Bridge was only a bridge. The stone path connecting the two cliffs, with fog surrounding it. Just a normal bridge.

"Terrible time, isn't it?" Xavier asked.

"Would not recommend," River agreed.

"But hey," Xavier continued, "you survived your first big Otherwoods challenge. That's amazing."

First? Every moment in The Otherwoods felt like a challenge.

River shook their head and sighed. "Barely."

They were frustrated with themself for almost turning back. But it had seemed so much like the real Avery. River gazed back at the empty bridge again, half expecting to see Avery standing there, betrayed and angry.

"What are you talking about?" Xavier put a hand on River's shoulder, and the color immediately faded. Xavier looked at River until they met his eyes. "You were very brave," he said. "Be proud of that."

It wasn't the first time someone had called River brave, but it might have been the first time they believed it, if just for a moment.

River wasn't sure if time passed differently on the bridge or what, but the usual gray of The Otherwoods felt darker, like night was already approaching.

"We should find a safe place to get some rest," Xavier said. "I don't know about you, but crossing that bridge took a lot out of me."

Xavier still looked haunted and emotional and River felt worse.

"Aren't we in the monsters' area?" River asked. "Is anywhere safe?"

"Isn't that the question?" Xavier muttered. He gave River a light smile. "There's a small river near here. Shockingly, the monsters don't really go around running water, as much as they seem to like you."

They weren't exactly pleased to be the only River monsters liked, but they would take the glimpse of safety.

"Okay," River said. "I can refill my water bottle too."

Tired of being held, Pancakes jumped to the ground, and the three set off in the direction of the river.

It was a temporary calm. River felt like something bad would happen soon after, but they tried to cast aside that thought.

Xavier touched one of the trees in stepping over a fallen branch, and River couldn't help but notice the bark was unaffected. Had they just imagined it lighting up at their touch earlier?

River reached toward the closest tree trunk, and its branches almost shivered in response, stretching back toward River. Sure enough, when their fingertips pressed against the bark, it glowed the same blue as before.

"Why does it do this?" River asked. "All the trees here glow when I touch them."

Xavier glanced back at River and the glowing bark. "They're reacting to the life in you, nothing to worry about."

River frowned. "It didn't light up when Pancakes touched it, and he's alive," River said, gesturing at their cat, who ignored them both and pounced on a dead leaf.

"Cats are spiritual animals, remember? They are right at home in the spirit realms. Humans?" Xavier gave River a pointed look. "Not so much."

That made sense. The trees were reacting to what didn't quite belong. River wondered if Avery felt the same strange pull of The Otherwoods. Despite everything, she would probably find beauty in the blue light.

River hoped she was okay. They moved away from the tree, the branches shaking in protest.

"Let's just keep going before any monsters notice us," they said.

They jumped over a rock, Pancakes at their heels, to catch up with Xavier and keep in the direction of the river.

"What did you see on the bridge?" Xavier asked. "Besides Avery."

River gave them a look. "So asking how you died is rude, but asking about my biggest fears isn't?"

Xavier shrugged. "I never said *I* was polite."

Although a lot of the bridge experience felt very personal, Xavier did have to go through most of it with them. Without him, they might not have been able to get through it at all. Besides, Xavier had opened up to them before, and never judged them. Not really. If they could tell anyone, it was him.

"It tried to scare me with some monsters from home," River admitted.

"Charles?" Xavier asked.

River nodded. "Charles is an actual monster, but there was another one too. One of my teachers."

"Ugh. I don't remember a lot, but I remember I hated school. I was so bad at tests."

River smiled a little. "I am too."

Xavier tilted his head. "Is this teacher really that scary? They're only human."

"Sure, but sometimes that's scarier. How she can hate me so much when she doesn't know me, and I can't even stand up for myself." River bit their lip.

"You can't be brave all the time," Xavier said softly.

"And maybe dealing with these monsters here will help you when you get back home."

A small silence grew between the two, only the sounds of twigs snapping and leaves crackling filling the air. River noticed that more bloodstains coated the trees on this side of the bridge. That wasn't good. But there were no signs of monsters yet.

"What did you see on the bridge?" It was only fair for River to ask. Xavier had asked them first.

"Same thing I always do," Xavier said easily. "Nothing."

River's jaw nearly hit the forest floor. It didn't matter if Xavier was a ghost, they couldn't believe that. "You're not afraid of anything?" they asked dubiously. "You seemed scared!"

"No, I'm afraid of *nothing*, it's totally different." Xavier looked away from River, focusing on the trees in front of him. "I'm afraid of not existing. Of my mind not working. Of there being nothing else. When I'm on the bridge, I can't see my body, or feel anything. It's almost like I don't exist."

River had never really thought about that. It sounded scary when Xavier put it that way, but there were so many *somethings* to be afraid of, they didn't understand how *nothing* could be worse.

"Aren't you already dead, though?" River asked. "Death isn't the end, then."

Xavier's expression was hard to read. Partly because he wasn't really looking at River and partly because there seemed to be too many emotions playing across his face.

"Maybe," Xavier said. "But maybe not." He swallowed.

"I don't have any way to really know I exist right now. What about when I pass on to whatever is next? No one who passes on comes back to the spirit realms, so there's no way to know what happens then. I don't know . . . maybe us once-human spirits are more like an echo. And what do echoes do? They fade into nothing."

That was a lot to process all at once. But River was glad that Xavier was still being so honest with them. Even if River didn't really know how to make the situation better like Xavier always seemed to.

"That's deep," River teased. Xavier gave them a little shove. "No, I mean . . . I don't know what'll happen. Maybe no one is supposed to know? So I can't really say much about that . . ." River took a big breath, trying to think of ways to shape the thoughts in their head into the right words, the ones that always felt more out of reach. "Maybe I don't know what it's like to wonder if I exist, but I do know what it's like to wonder why I do. Honestly, there's a lot of people who like to pretend I don't."

River knew that in part, this was an effect of them trying to blend into the background as much as possible. Sometimes, River felt only as real as the people who acknowledged them. But when someone tries their best to not be noticed, everyone around them will eventually follow suit. River spent so much time alone, were they really all that different from the spirits and monsters that no one else believed in?

Plus, there was their identity on top of it.

Plenty of people like Ms. Deery didn't believe that there

were more than two genders, despite all the evidence. No one had believed that River could see spirits, no one had believed that monsters existed, despite all the evidence. Despite River themself knowing with everything in them that both of these things were true.

But that was the danger.

When enough people don't believe you, it is so much harder to hold on to that brilliant light that is the belief in yourself.

It was hard for River to hold on to it, but they had to.

Especially in The Otherwoods, in all its terrifying proof. And if River didn't have their identity, the things that made them happy, they'd have nothing to believe in at all. And believing was what had saved them their whole life.

"That's ridiculous," Xavier finally said. "You're nonbinary because you say you're nonbinary. Why should people question it?"

River shrugged. "I don't know. I know that's who I am. If all these people say it's not real, that it's something for attention, or I'm just confused . . . well, then, doesn't that mean they don't think I'm real? Because if there are only two gender options, then I wouldn't exist. I'd be nothing too, right?"

"But you're not nothing," Xavier said. He almost seemed upset, stopping to turn to River and grab both their arms. "You're someone, and you're someone special. I mean, you came all the way here to save your friend. That's impressive, that's . . . magic." There was a strange look on his face when he said that word, but it disappeared as quickly as it had appeared. "And even if you weren't, you're a person. With likes and fears and hopes. That's enough to exist."

River was suddenly aware of their heart fluttering in their chest, but for once, not out of fear. No one had ever said those kinds of things to them before, not like that. It made River want to pull Xavier in for a hug. He was like the older brother River had never had; it was like the sibling dynamic River had only read about. Teasing, sure, but there for them when they needed it. Understanding in a way that their parents just couldn't be.

River didn't realize how much they needed those words until Xavier said them, and they wanted to give him kind words in return.

Because River's first impression was right. Xavier was a hero.

"What about you?" River asked. "With your likes and fears and hopes?" River brushed off Xavier's hands, but smiled. "I can't explain any of this. I mean, I barely passed my science class this year, and I still have time to fail, you know, if I don't die here." River swallowed. They were getting off topic. "But what I do know is that you do exist, and you made it all the way here, and you'll make it all the way through whatever comes after."

River could tell that Xavier was really thinking about what they said. It was nice to be listened to. Even Pancakes looked back at them as he stayed close but sniffed around and scratched his claws on the trees.

River had to admit, at least to themself, that they were

grateful they'd run into Xavier. Everything would have been much worse, if not impossible, had they been alone.

Xavier took a shaky breath. "Regardless, I'm glad you were there. If I hadn't been able to see you, I'm not sure I would've made it."

"Me neither," River said. "Maybe we do make a good team."

Xavier laughed a little. "You know, when all this is done, I think I'll actually miss you, River."

River smiled. "Of course. I'm pretty great."

Xavier rolled his eyes. "I take it back. I won't miss you at all."

But, despite their best efforts, River knew they'd miss him too.

19

The Other River

They didn't need to travel much farther after that to reach the river, and it was a welcome sight compared with the rest of The Otherwoods. It wasn't wide, maybe about Cursed Bridge length, but it stretched on, cutting through the ground. Some flowers grew along the edges, and unlike The City of Souls dead foliage, they were flourishing and full of life.

The dense trees still loomed behind them, but the air felt that little bit fresher, smelling more like wet rocks and maple. It was comforting, maybe even safe. It was truly like the river was untouched by the monsters and for that reason, was able to keep some of its light. It was the perfect spot to stay for the night. Or at least, as perfect as one could get outside The City of Souls.

As the world around them grew darker, and when they could no longer see beyond the top layer of trees, the gentle trickle at the river's edge remained a calming melody. Even the bed of moss that River rested on, their backpack an unfortunate pillow, felt a little softer.

Having already drunk his fill and peed by a tree, Pancakes was stretched out near River. He was deep in sleep, whiskers and paws twitching as he ignored the world around him. River resisted the urge to pet his gray fur. It would only wake up the cat, and after what they all went through, Pancakes more than deserved a good rest.

River did too, but somehow, they were having a lot more trouble.

"Can't sleep?" Xavier asked, voice not much above a whisper.

"No," River said. Their voice cut through the quiet night. "You?"

"I literally can't sleep, I'm a spirit."

"Oh." River glanced over at Xavier. "Sucks."

"Yeah."

Despite not being able to ever sleep, Xavier had made himself a nice little bed in a mossy, floral overgrowth. River thought it made him look oddly pretty, but figured that wasn't always something a boy wanted to hear.

"Do you ever miss being alive?" Immediately after the words escaped River's lips, they regretted them. Of course he missed being alive. That had to be as rude as asking about his death.

"Well, you know I certainly miss ice cream."

It was a fair answer to a not totally fair question.

"Remember when you said you were chasing after someone?" River asked.

"I say a lot of things," Xavier snapped. After a few moments of only the slow-moving water murmuring, he gave a softer, "Yeah."

River looked back up at the sky. There were no stars in The Otherwoods. That wasn't as unsettling as it should've been. Living near a city, River never saw stars anyway.

The missing moon, however, made them feel a little lonely.

It was like turning the page of a book and seeing that the next ten were blank. Something wasn't quite right. River felt that way a lot, but it was much worse since they'd passed through that portal.

They wanted their bed, with an actual pillow. They wanted the safety of their parents in the other room. They even wanted the smell of oatmeal that drifted up the stairs in the morning that River and their dad always complained about.

They missed all of it.

Talking to Xavier, at least, was a distraction.

"Who are you chasing after?" River asked.

Xavier turned his head to look at River, crushing a flower with his cheek. "You're a pretty nosy kid, aren't you?"

"I prefer the term 'inquisitive.'"

Even through the darkness, River could see Xavier's eyes roll.

"My little brother," Xavier said finally. "He reminds me of you—you're both annoying."

River decided not to comment on that, because it was clear they were touching an emotional topic. River knew they were no more annoying than Xavier was himself. They didn't want to admit it to him now, but it did make them happy that Xavier thought of them like a sibling, since they felt the same way.

River wondered what Xavier's brother looked like. If he liked to tease like Xavier did or if he was more serious. If, in some impossible circumstances, the three of them would all get along.

"What's his name?"

Xavier's eyes were glassy. "I don't remember. Faces stick around more for me, but names . . . I told you. They start to slip away." River didn't know what to say to that. No one would. There were some sentences that didn't have a correct response. The sounds echoed in the air and faded away, but the meaning of them stuck, trapped behind. Xavier forced a little smile. "Let's call him the Other River, since you are both so *inquisitive*."

He was lucky he was too far away for River to shove him.

"What was Other River like?" River asked.

"He was smart, curious, liked to explore. But he was usually in his own little world. Sometimes, I was pretty sure I was the only one he let in it . . ." Xavier snorted. "Here I am, talking about him in the past tense when I'm the dead one."

River decided they would like Other River, and it was

nice that they reminded Xavier of him. It was a comfort when they didn't have much else.

"I guess the real world is past tense here," River said. "Since The Otherwoods is our present."

"I guess so." Xavier turned his face back to the sky. Near the river, it was free from all the bent branches, so they had a clearer view of the seemingly endless purple-black. "I hope he's okay. That's why I have to wait for him. He's always relied on me. I can't have him go through the afterlife alone."

River shifted on the moss. "I don't want to be rude, but . . . how do you know he won't go to The Elsewhere?"

"Because he was like you in that way too. Magic." Xavier swallowed. "He didn't see monsters or spirits, but he *felt* things. He would know if something bad was going to happen, sometimes he'd have dreams before things happened." Xavier's eyes were up toward the inky-black sky where the stars should be, almost like his brother was looking at the same one. "If everyone's right about why we ended up in The Otherwoods, he'll definitely come here too."

"Maybe he won't have any regrets?" River suggested hopefully.

"He has me," Xavier said. "The one bad thing he couldn't predict."

River was silent for a moment. They'd never thought that much about people like them, or sort of like them. If there were others who had psychic abilities like Natalia and Xavier's brother, did that mean there were others who had supernatural abilities like River?

"Is that why you want to wait for him?" River asked.

"He has to know it isn't his fault," Xavier said. "Besides, he's not the type of person who can be alone, you know? Our parents were gone a lot, and I remember he'd always come to my room, so we could play video games or so I could help with homework, anything to have someone else around. Or when he had nightmares, those bad predictions, he'd bring his pillow into my room and sleep on the floor. He was just someone who hated to be alone." His voice was tight and almost pained. "Since I died, I don't know who's there for him, and I hate it. Maybe that's what I need to pass on, and we can do it together. I can't let him be alone again . . . not when we're faced with the possibility of nothing." As if sensing the fear in his voice, Xavier cleared his throat. "I'll do anything to make sure that doesn't happen."

The way Xavier sounded almost made River wish they really had a sibling. Someone who cared that much about them.

Almost like he could read minds, Pancakes nuzzled into River's side before falling back asleep. River cracked a little smile no one could see.

Someone *else* who cared that much, they amended.

"I'm an only child," River said. "So it's just me." They glanced at the sleeping cat, who put his paws over his face. "Well, and Pancakes."

Xavier chuckled.

"I can wait for you too, since you'll probably end up back here," Xavier said. "Then you wouldn't have to be alone."

There was something so sad in his voice. River figured

he didn't like talking about death very much, and they couldn't blame Xavier. They didn't want to think about that kind of thing, but the idea of having something after, someone waiting for them . . .

It was nice.

"And Pancakes," Xavier added.

River laughed. "Thanks," they said. "I'd like that."

River's intestines took that moment to grumble. They couldn't give River one nice moment before causing another struggle.

"I have to go to the bathroom," River said. "Keep an eye on Pancakes."

Normally, they would have been terrified to go alone, but having to bring everyone and all their things seemed like a lot. Not to mention, they really didn't want Xavier to *hear* them.

If they were able to survive The Cursed Bridge, they could survive going to the bathroom alone.

"Number one or two?" River glared at Xavier, who shrugged. "I want a sense of how long you'll take."

River unzipped their backpack to grab the toilet paper, flashlight, hand sanitizer, and pocketknife—just in case. "It'll be a minute."

"Don't go far, and scream really loudly if anything happens."

"That should be easy enough."

With Pancakes still asleep, River flicked on their flashlight and headed to a nearby spot covered by some trees. They braced themself for what they had to do.

Books and movies always talked about adventure, but none of them talked about pooping in the woods.

The added discomfort of monsters able to appear at any time didn't help.

River finished as quickly as they could, put a mound of dirt on top like they were Pancakes, and sanitized their hands. When they were finished, they breathed a sigh of relief. If River had to die in The Otherwoods, they really didn't want it to be while they were using the (outdoor) bathroom. They also took a moment to thank Past River for prioritizing toilet paper.

After pocketing the hand sanitizer and knife, they held the toilet paper in one hand and the flashlight in the other. It might have been a smarter idea to hold the knife, but the toilet paper wouldn't fit in their pocket. Adventuring really wasn't glamorous.

Something red on the ground caught their eye, and River dropped their flashlight to look.

A bright red trail of dripping blood was on the dirt.

Normally, this was the exact type of thing that River would have ignored. That was a major rule they lived by: If they saw a trail of blood, they certainly wouldn't follow it. They would run in the other direction and probably never come that way again.

Except the trail of blood was in the direction of the river.

River's heart jumped right into their throat, and they walked faster. What if something bad had happened to Xavier? Or to Pancakes? River didn't know what they would do if their cat was harmed. Panic rose in their stomach, and they burned with the immediate need to see Pancakes and make sure he was okay.

Obviously, River didn't want Xavier harmed either, but they were pretty sure spirits didn't bleed, so the concern had to be for their fluffy best friend.

But the blood stopped at the edge of the trees. River could see Xavier, petting Pancakes at the side of the water. There was a short distance between them still, but neither of the two seemed bloodied. River looked behind them, around the trees, but they didn't see any sign of a monster, or anything else disturbing or out of place.

Using the flashlight, they caught the end of the blood trail, and saw that it led to one particular tree. It was close to the edge of the forest, with the little riverside campsite they'd set up in clear view of it.

River traced the trail up the tree, and their heart stopped.

In blood, there was a large message written on the bark. *THEY ARE WAITING.*

Underneath, a small note was pinned. The handwriting seemed to be an exact match of the warning they had received back at the inn.

River put the flashlight directly on the slip of paper.

Keep going, and you won't make it out alive.

20

The Threat of Monsters

River couldn't help themself. They screamed. A short, quick one, but enough to alert a sleeping cat and a sleepless spirit. Both Xavier and Pancakes rushed over to River.

"What is it?" Xavier asked.

River had to swallow their panic as they pointed to the message on the tree. "Someone did this and left another note."

River handed it over to Xavier, who read it with a concerned expression. Finally, the spirit looked back at River. "Don't worry about it."

It wasn't what River expected to hear. "Threats written in blood seem like something to worry about."

"Normally, yes," Xavier agreed. "But this looks like the

work of a vengeful spirit. They probably want to stop you from saving Avery."

River hadn't thought of anyone other than the monsters wanting to stop them. What was in it for those spirits if River didn't find Avery?

"Why?" they managed to ask.

"They're vengeful," Xavier answered. "They're like that."

River wasn't sure that was the best answer. Xavier was smart and heroic. It didn't feel right that he wanted to ignore something like this. Especially not when it was the second strange note River had received. Maybe Xavier was hiding something from them because he thought they couldn't handle it?

"Let me know if you get anything else like this, but I promise it'll be okay," Xavier continued. "With Pancakes here, they can't hurt you."

River nodded, but they didn't feel much better about it.

Still, the three returned to their camping spot, and River lay back down on their mossy bed. They really couldn't sleep most of the night, but pretended to so Xavier wouldn't worry.

Once the morning brightened again, they got ready to head out. Pancakes was happily finishing off the packet of tuna River had given him for breakfast. River managed to eat a leftover cookie from the inn and a granola bar they'd brought. They weren't exactly the healthiest of options, but River was certain their mom would understand given the circumstances.

Regardless, Mom and Dad would be so mad about

River running away in the first place, a few breakfast cookies would be the least of their concerns.

But whatever punishment River would receive at home didn't seem worth thinking about. Especially not when the idea of home made their eyes water and their heart ache. None of that mattered then. Today was the day they were getting Avery and getting the heck out of The Otherwoods. It had to be.

"How far are we from The Centertrees now?" River asked Xavier as they repacked their bag and prepared to continue the journey.

"Not too far," Xavier said. "There's really just one more major obstacle we have to get through."

One more obstacle didn't sound too bad, but River couldn't bring themself to be hopeful.

"One obstacle . . . like The Cursed Bridge?" River asked.

Xavier snorted, brushing away the comment with his hands. "No, it's nothing like The Cursed Bridge."

That made River feel a little better about the whole situati—

"It's *so* much worse," Xavier went on.

Oh. Well.

River gulped, sweat prickling their palms. They may have made it across the bridge, but they weren't sure how much worse they could handle. "So much worse" wasn't promising.

"Why?" River asked. "What is it?"

Xavier must've noticed the tremble in River's voice. It matched the way their arms shook on their backpack straps. "I think it's better you find out when we get there, okay?"

Xavier probably thought if River knew the danger, they would want to give up and run away. River would've liked to be able to defend themself, but they were pretty sure they agreed.

If their imagination thought the worst, the actual obstacle wouldn't seem so bad in comparison.

If it didn't . . . well, maybe they were better off simply not knowing.

"Ready?" Xavier asked.

"No." River picked up Pancakes. "Now I am. Let's go."

Unfortunately, the river didn't lead in the direction of The Centertrees, so they had to leave the peaceful shore behind and return to the forest. Despite Xavier's assurance, from the moment River saw the note left in the tree, their gut had grown heavy with the feeling something bad would happen. With each step they took into the woods, that feeling continued to grow.

By the river, the world was quiet aside from the water.

Back in the forest, the world around them was alive.

There were growls, caws, rattles, and titters. None of them sounded quite right, like they would belong in the real world. They came in notes that were sharps or flats, something almost familiar but not quite.

Not close, but not far, sounding like they rang in from every direction.

Before, River had fearfully anticipated a monster appearing, but now, they waited for a monster to strike. Monsters were clearly around, stalking from a distance. Every shadowed corner or sudden movement caused River to jump.

Everything felt like a threat.

"What do we do if we see a monster?" River asked.

"Try not to die," Xavier answered. "You've managed it before."

River tried to focus on the things they did like about Xavier, because they were very hard to remember in that moment.

"I thought you would have something a little more specific," River said. "Like a clear way to stop them."

"Same way you stop anything: you kill it."

"How do you kill it?" River asked.

"Same way you kill anything."

"That's not exactly easy when they all seem built specifically to eat you."

Xavier gave an empty smile. "And that's why they're a problem. Try to have some weapon on hand."

So much for any actual plan. At least River had their pocketknife.

Although they didn't have much of a choice since they had to keep up with Xavier, River tried their best to be light on their feet. Their footsteps weren't entirely silent, but they weren't so loud they stood out against the rest of the noise around them.

River didn't feel like they could breathe properly, they were so waiting for something to happen.

If we can just make it to the obstacle, River thought, *I think we'll be okay.*

They didn't pretend they'd be okay after that point, and they still didn't know what the obstacle was. Maybe what Xavier considered worse wasn't that bad?

Unlikely, River knew, but one can only be so much of a realist in a fantasy realm.

If we can just make it . . .

Something scurried in front of them, a thin, shadowy creature that moved like a lizard but had feathers sprouting from its tail. It ran off into the distance.

Time almost stopped for a second, as River's eyes locked on the feathers. Pancakes immediately shot off after the creature, completely in the wrong direction from where they were headed.

River's stomach dropped.

They didn't even think, they just ran.

21

The Pawsitively Perfect
Mr. Fluffy Pancakes

There weren't that many things River truly and deeply cared about, but Pancakes was one of them. Aside from their parents, the gray cat was at the top of the list. River hadn't known Pancakes since they were born, but they'd known Pancakes since they really knew themself, which was basically the equivalent.

Pancakes might've been just a cat, but he was the cat that was always there for River. He accepted River for who they really were, and never saw them as anything different. He protected River as best as he could, from Charles and from River's own negative thoughts. He was there to soak up the tears, to cuddle away the fears, to sit on River's face in the morning and meow for breakfast.

Okay, maybe that last part wasn't ideal, but it was all part of Pancakes' charm.

River couldn't let anything happen to Pancakes. They *wouldn't*.

They couldn't outrun the cat either, but they tried. They ran as fast as their legs would take them, trying to keep sight of the streak of gray fur. They lost Pancakes when he ran through a small area of dead overgrowth, and River's entire body filled with panic.

But they kept going.

Despite Xavier's calls behind them, and the branch ends that pulled at their skin and made little cuts on their face, they kept going.

Finally, in a small clearing between trees, River caught up with Pancakes. He had his claws dug into the small creature and was happily chewing on its feathery tail.

"It had to be feathers," River muttered.

Pancakes looked up at River, allowing the creature to get away. He didn't try to follow it this time, because River had already scooped up the cat and pulled him into a hug. Pancakes squirmed, but seemed to understand that this was very important to River, because he let it happen anyway.

River closed their eyes and focused on the feeling of the cat's warm fur against their face. "Don't scare me like that, you jerk."

Pancakes hissed.

"Excuse me, did you just—" River opened their eyes. Pancakes was looking past River. Their heart pounded in their chest, skin starting to crawl. River turned slowly, to stare right into the narrowed eyes of a large monster.

It was twice the size of Charles, looming over the two of them. The bottom half of it was tree-like, with a wide body that erupted into dark tentacles. The tentacles oozed an inky substance that stained the blades of grass beneath. The top half was more along the lines of an angler fish, with a strange spiked antenna. But instead of a large mouth, there was simply a hole lined with rows and rows of narrow, spiked teeth.

The situation was very, very bad.

At first, the monster looked like it would turn away. But then it paused. From somewhere in the forest, there were hisses and rattles. It almost sounded like . . . a conversation.

Are the monsters somehow communicating?

The thought died as the monster twisted back to River, eyes wild and straining. River's vision clouded at the edges.

The monster roared, and when it did, three thin tentacles shot out of its mouth hole toward them. River managed to move out of the way at the last second, and the tentacles slammed into the dirt before retreating into the depths of the creature. Pancakes spilled out of their arms and landed on his feet a yard away.

Pancakes was okay, but River still had to worry about themself.

They scrambled to grab the knife from their pocket, their hands shaking so badly they almost dropped it twice. Their grip was slippery with sweat, but they got the knife in front of them in a defensive position. When they pulled out the blade, it didn't look like it would do much damage.

It was maybe three inches long, and the monster was more than double their height.

But they held on to it because it was all they had.

Would they be able to do it? Would they stand a chance against a monster like that without Xavier? They had no choice but to try.

River faced it, legs shaking.

Despite the way it looked, the creature wasn't slow, and it twisted its gruesome body toward River. It widened its jaws and shot out the tentacles. River wasn't quite fast enough, and the tentacles slammed into their stomach, knocking them onto the ground.

With their free hand, River held their stomach, choking for air.

The monster moved closer, saliva dripping from its teeth.

River was frozen in fear.

Then, puffed out to twice his size, back arched and teeth bared, Pancakes stepped between River and the monster. Pancakes hissed.

And then launched himself at the monster.

The cat dug his claws into the top of the monster's head, swiping across an eye. The creature groaned in pain and used two of its tentacles to toss the cat away. Pancakes smacked against the ground. River's heart lurched, and they tasted bile.

"Pancakes!"

The cat looked up at River, eyes wide.

He was okay. But it didn't matter. River was shaking. With the knife in their hand, they slowly stood.

"Nobody hurts Mr. Fluffy Pancakes," River said.

Then they let out a yell as they charged into the monster. The blade plunged into the monster but didn't go deep. River kept pushing, until their arm was fully pressed into the monster's flesh, and started slicing. Tentacles grabbed their wrist, but filled with an anger that overcame their fear, River kept digging the blade farther and farther into the monster.

Finally, a swell of the inky ooze poured over River's torso, and the monster crumpled to the ground.

River stepped away, completely covered in the shiny ink. Did they just do that?

A laugh escaped from River. They'd defeated a monster.

"Well, that was certainly something," Xavier said. River turned toward his voice and saw him sitting with Pancakes on his lap. "Pancakes is all good, by the way."

"Why do you always show up right *after* the monster attack?" River asked.

Xavier shrugged. "Either I'm very lucky or you're very unlucky."

With all their heart, River truly believed the latter.

"Quite the mess you made there," Xavier continued. He smiled. "I'm proud of you."

River felt a bit proud of themself too. Mostly, they were glad that Pancakes was okay, but it also was nice to know that they did it. They slayed a scary monster. And without any help, really. Maybe they were a little capable after all.

Maybe more than a little.

The excitement from the fight faded as the feeling of

the cold inky slime caught up with them, and River's stomach already ached from the tentacle hit.

Swallowing the urge to puke, River turned to Xavier. "Any chance you have a change of underwear?"

22

The Connection
Between Them

Not only did Xavier have a change of underwear, he also had a full change of clothes in the small bag he kept on his shoulders. It took the entire pack of flushable wipes River had brought along (just in case) to get all the goo off. Then they hid behind a tree to change into new clothes, leaving the soiled ones behind.

They now wore a comfortable pair of gray sweatpants that weren't too heavy and a plain tank top with another zip-up hoodie. Their fingernails were still stained with the inky substance, but they'd done the best they could.

"Thanks," River said to Xavier when they had themself together.

He had used the very last of the wipes to clean off

River's knife. He handed it back to them. "No worries, I don't need much with me, so I'm glad I came prepared."

"I won't count on it in the future," River said, taking the knife.

Xavier grinned. "You really shouldn't."

Pancakes sniffed at the pile of dirty wipes and made a disgusted face. Now that they were no longer covered in the mess, River scooped up the cat and pulled him into another hug. "I'm so glad you're okay, Pancakes."

"Isn't it 'Mr. Fluffy Pancakes'?" Xavier asked.

River's face felt fiery as they looked away from him. "Shut up."

"I think it's cute."

"No one asked what you think."

Also seemingly happy that both of them had survived, Pancakes purred in River's arms. Xavier reached out to scratch his ears, but a low growl escaped from the cat.

"That's what you get for making fun of his name," River said.

Xavier looked a little hurt. "It's really more embarrassing for River, Pancakes."

Pancakes hissed at Xavier before tucking his head back into River's armpit.

"Wow," River said to Xavier, wearing a bigger smile than he had while teasing them. "Just wow."

Xavier brushed them both off. "Are we ready to get moving again? We're a little off course now, but still not far."

To the big, scary obstacle they still had to face. Right.

River wasn't looking forward to that.

"I don't know why you keep asking," River said. "I'm never ready."

"But you go anyway, and that's what counts." Xavier patted them on the shoulder despite a very pained glare from Pancakes.

With the knife in their pocket and their backpack secure, River adjusted Pancakes to a better position. "All right, let's do it."

They felt bad about leaving behind the stained wipes and clothing, but they didn't have much of an option. Their backpack was already full, and Pancakes was enough of an added weight. They really couldn't afford to carry trash with them, even if it made River want to apologize to every tree.

Xavier started back in the direction they'd come from, and River followed close behind him. While they still didn't want to face whatever would come next, being lost in a forest full of monsters wasn't exactly their idea of a good time either.

It was possible the commotion and resulting monster carcass had scared off some of the other predators. Although the background growls and howls started up again, they didn't seem to come any closer. They remained at a distance, like some strange music.

They were there, though. And they were watching. River could feel their gazes.

They needed to get their mind off it, relax their muscles so they'd have some energy left for whatever horror they'd later face.

"Do you really think Avery's okay?" River asked Xavier.

Probably not the best question to get their mind off things, as they were worried about her, but they were trying.

"I really do," Xavier said. "This might not make you feel better, but you're the special one. The monsters won't hurt her if they want you."

"I don't want to be special," River answered. "And I don't know why they want me."

If it meant that Avery was safe, it was a good thing, but only for that. River hoped that she wouldn't give up, that she knew River would come for her. Somehow.

Xavier shrugged. "I'm not sure what to tell you, kid. We'll have to find out. It's the way it is. You can see spirits and monsters. You were destined for an interesting life."

Or doomed, but River didn't say that. They adjusted Pancakes in their arms again—although he was just a cat, he was heavy—and kept moving forward.

River wondered how the monsters knew not to hurt Avery, and thought back to that moment with the last one. How it looked to the trees for some answer and seemed to find it buried in the growls and snarls.

"Can the monsters talk to each other?" River asked.

Xavier nodded. "I don't know how to explain it, but the monsters are all connected. What do they call it? Hive mind? Like how bees don't talk to each other, but they're all on the same page of protecting the queen?"

River understood that, and they'd heard of the concept,

but the thought of a monster hive mind was more than a little unsettling.

"Who's the queen, then?" River asked.

Xavier looked over at River, shadows in his normally light eyes. "Well, The Otherwoods."

River lifted an eyebrow. "That's a place. How can a place tell the monsters what to do?"

Xavier laughed. "Funny, coming from the one human who sees impossible things all the time." He gave an over-dramatic shrug, but there was still a strange shine in his eyes. "It's so much more than a place. It's magic, River. I don't have the answers to everything."

River frowned. They didn't expect Xavier to have the answers to everything, but they hoped he had the answers to everything they wanted to know about. There was so much about The Otherwoods and their involvement in it that didn't make sense to them. If the monsters—or The Otherwoods themselves—wanted them here, what did they want them *for*?

Clearly it was important enough to try to lure in River throughout their whole life, and with the increase in portal and monster activity in recent weeks, there had to be a bigger, more urgent reason for why now. Especially if it was enough to take Avery and use her as bait to get to River.

What did that mean for when River found her?

They swallowed. They'd have to face it just like the bridge, and the last monster.

Like Xavier said, they'd figure it out.

They could only hope they'd like the answer when they did. Although River knew enough to expect otherwise.

"You do know what the next obstacle is, though," River said. "You might as well tell me that. We're almost there, aren't we?"

"Yeah," Xavier said. "You really want to know?"

River nodded.

"They call it The Monsters' Den," Xavier said.

That was an unlucky-sounding name. Maybe River *didn't* want to know more.

"Okay," River said. "Good to know." They looked down at Pancakes, who had his eyes closed and seemed very content. River wished they could do the same, but they didn't seem capable of being that calm. They looked back at Xavier. "Is it okay to still be a little scared?"

Xavier's lips twisted into a reassuring smile. "Honestly, it'd be strange if you weren't."

23

The Monsters' Den

River hadn't known what to expect when they made it to the area of The Otherwoods known as The Monsters' Den, but it didn't really matter either. Whatever image their mind had conjured up was nothing compared with the horror in front of them.

At the edge of The Monsters' Den, the forest floor abruptly dipped into a jagged cliff, but the drop wasn't more than ten feet. River could easily see the bottom, which was much worse than not seeing it. They wished they could travel back in time to the moments they couldn't.

Monsters filled the bottom of the valley. All different shapes and sizes, in shades of gray from a smoky white to an inky black, they slithered and stomped around below.

Only patches of dirt were visible, the concentration of monsters was so high. They bit and clawed at each other, staining the ground with their dark blood, black in some cases and a deep red in others. The noise of them was overwhelming, a constant cacophony of snarls, growls, and roars. What were they all doing down there? Was it a place where monsters were born, or where they went to die? It was hard to tell their age or condition other than frightening and better-left-alone.

More importantly, how in the spirit world were River and Xavier supposed to cross it?

It was a rift similar to the one below The Cursed Bridge, but there was no bridge here. Only jagged rock leading to a drop, with claws and teeth snapping at the bottom.

River never thought they'd consider experiencing the bridge again, but compared to this, the illusions seemed like a piece of cake.

"How are we supposed to get across?" River asked.

"No idea," Xavier said with a smile. "That's why we need a plan."

River wanted to let Pancakes claw the smile off his face. "Haven't you done this before?"

"Well, it's a little easier when you're already dead."

It wasn't the answer River wanted, but they had to admit it made sense. The monsters couldn't kill a spirit, so it's likely those teeth and claws wouldn't have much of an effect on the already deceased.

They would have a horrible effect on River and Pancakes, though.

"Do you have any ideas?" River asked.

Xavier stood right at the edge of the ravenous ravine. He looked back and forth between the two edges, eyes skimming over the monsters filling the middle. "It's certainly too large to jump . . ."

"Of course it's too large to jump!" River had too much fear in their body to leave any room for patience.

Xavier gave them a look. "Excuse me, River. It's called brainstorming. I'm getting the bad ideas out of my system first, and then I'll be able to come up with good ones."

"I'm not sure that's how brainstorming works," River said.

"It's exactly how brainstorming works," Xavier countered. "We think through why the bad ideas won't work, and if none of those reasons apply to a new idea, it has to be the right one." He gave River a pat on the head. "It's okay, they don't teach this kind of thing in elementary school."

"I'm in *middle school*." River was certain Xavier remembered exactly how old they were; he was just making it a point to get on their nerves. The teasing was annoying enough usually, but it really wasn't the time. Xavier *was* like an older brother. River sighed. "Whatever. Get the rest of the bad ideas out, then."

Xavier put his hand on his chin and started to pace back and forth. His eyebrows were scrunched together, leaving a deep single line between the two. River had to admit to themself that he looked very intelligent.

Or, perhaps, a little constipated.

Either way, he was essentially their biggest hope.

"Making a glider to fly across . . . we don't have anything to chop down trees . . . materials would be a hassle, so no. Trying to fight through the monsters . . . we're way outnumbered and only have one small weapon, so no. Offering up Pancakes as sacrifice . . ."

Pancakes and River glared at Xavier.

He put his hands up. "That was a joke!"

River sighed and sat down. It was a small relief to have the weight of their backpack off their shoulders, the ground supporting it instead. Pancakes curled up on their lap, taking his opportunity for a quick nap.

"If we could chop down a tree, do you think it would be tall enough to fall across and make a bridge?" Xavier asked.

River tilted their head back, feeling their hair brush against the backpack. "We're going to die here, aren't we?"

"Maybe with that attitude," Xavier said.

River forced a smile. "We're probably going to die here, but maybe not?"

"That's the spirit!" Xavier walked behind them, bent down, and unzipped River's backpack. "You have to have something in here that'd be useful . . ."

"Thanks for asking to look through my stuff."

Xavier stopped rummaging to peek around and give River a look. "You asked me how I *died*."

River rolled their eyes. "Apparently, you'll keep reminding me about that until *I* die."

"Even after, once you meet with me and Other River to pass on."

It was endearing and annoying at the same time. River

gave up and let Xavier continue looking. Maybe it would spark an idea for them. River didn't think they had anything embarrassing inside.

Although in that moment, they were doubting themself.

The buzz of the monsters grew a little bit louder. It was like surround sound—the noise wasn't just coming from the den below, but all around them. River covered their ears, but it didn't help much—the sound kept ringing in River's head. They couldn't escape it; it was like it was in their mind. River hoped Xavier would come up with something soon so they could get as far away from the sound as possible. Feeling like there were monsters in your brain wasn't exactly pleasant.

"Yes! This is it!" Xavier exclaimed.

River tried to turn around and look, but with Xavier holding the backpack and the backpack still on River's back, they couldn't exactly move. "What is it?"

Xavier zipped up their backpack and moved to face them. He held the coiled rope that River brought along in his hands.

"We can use this to get up and down the edges," Xavier said. "Jumping might hurt."

River looked down at the length of the drop. Jumping would probably hurt, although the impossible amount of monsters at the bottom would hurt a lot more.

"I mean, sure," River said. "But that doesn't help us get across." They uncoiled the rope. It wasn't thick but was very long. "Too bad we can't just climb across."

They looked at the rope and then at the nightmarish valley.

River gulped. "I have an idea, and I think it might work," they said, "but I really don't like it."

Xavier smiled.

24

The Balancing Act

River had been right about one thing: they did not like the idea. But it was all they had, and as terrible as it sounded, neither of them could think of a better option. So they went for it. Xavier put on River's backpack with Pancakes inside, wrapped in River's hoodie like a little burrito. The backpack was zipped around Pancakes, allowing his head to stick out for air.

The rope had cleared out a lot of space.

Pancakes wasn't happy, but he knew how to read the room, so he didn't complain.

River tied one end of the rope tightly to the closest tree on their end. River had a cousin who always hung out at indoor climbing gyms and had showed River how to tie some knots. So River used the figure-eight follow-through and finished it off with a stopper knot.

Actually trying rock climbing had been too terrifying for them, but their cousin and the other climbers were very nice. River was put on belay a few times, so they had a good memory for tying knots. At least it had proved useful.

Xavier grabbed the rest of the rope.

"You sure you'll be okay?" River asked.

"It's not me I'm worried about," Xavier said—like River needed to hear that.

They rolled their eyes to hide their fear and kissed the sour-faced Pancakes on the top of his head.

And so, Part One of River's Reluctant Plan commenced.

River could only wait by the edge and hope that Pancakes would keep quiet. They didn't know if being in the backpack would be enough of a cover, but they hoped Xavier would be able to protect him if anything happened.

Maybe it wasn't a good idea to leave the cat in the spirit's hands after that sacrifice comment . . .

It was too late to worry about it at that point. Xavier was already climbing down the side of the cliff, using the rope to slowly help him down. There was some relief in the fact that Pancakes didn't slip out of the backpack or start screaming, but River was nervous for the moment they'd touch ground.

With the relatively short drop, it wasn't long before Xavier was on both feet, and staring down a wall of monsters.

The one closest to him—a creature with sharp claws and a posture like a bear's—swiped at Xavier. River's heart leapt, feeling like it smacked against the edge of their rib cage. But the claws passed right through Xavier's body.

A bit of disappointment flashed through River.

Wait . . . They weren't disappointed, they were glad that Xavier was unharmed. What was wrong with them?

The monster buzzing grew louder, and River could barely hear their own thoughts. Were they somehow feeling the monster's emotions?

After the miss, the monster pretty much gave up. Others tried to grab Xavier, but like the first monster, they passed right through. None of them bothered with the backpack at all, too focused on the used-to-be-human spirit in front of them. As Xavier walked through the flood of monsters, he released more and more rope on the ground, creating a little trail behind him.

This wasn't the more intense part of the plan, but River could still barely believe it was working so well.

Xavier was almost the entire way across, and he still had plenty of rope left. The climb up would be harder, since he didn't have anything to help and needed to free-hand to the top. River had to remind themself to breathe.

It was harder to see from a distance, but River could make out Xavier taking his first step up the wall. His hands reached up, feeling for holds. He was already off the ground.

That had to be something.

Since Xavier was facing the wall, however, Pancakes was more exposed. One of the monsters, something like a stretched-out weasel with spiked tentacles for a face, approached the cat's head.

River swallowed their scream.

Pancakes was already annoyed and in no mood for a monster to bother him, apparently, because he hissed and bit down on one of the small tentacles.

The monster retreated, but the movement got the attention of the other ones nearby. Bigger ones, with tougher skin and sharper claws.

River's heart pounded in their chest, so loudly they could hardly hear anything else. How could they have let Pancakes go off without them? All they had was the pocketknife they'd tied to their pants with their sweatpants strings. There was no way they would get there in time to help, and even if they tried, at least twenty monsters would eat them first.

River felt it, the hunger of the monsters. It rose in their intestines and nestled in their stomach. It was loud and large, and they couldn't hear over the cursed buzzing.

But they had to do something.

Heart pounding wildly and sweat dripping from all over, River stood at the edge of the valley. They took a deep breath.

"HEY!" River called out. "It's me! The one you're all looking for!"

The buzzing shifted as the monsters turned in the direction of their voice. The hunger didn't go away completely but morphed into something familiar that River couldn't place. Worry?

Xavier used the opportunity to scramble up faster.

"That's right!" River jumped with their arms out,

trying to be as big and distracting as possible. "So come get me, you . . . ugly-faced scum!"

It wasn't the best insult, but it got the monsters' attention. Xavier climbed over the opposite edge, Pancakes unharmed on his back.

They were safe. Even if the world still didn't quiet, and River couldn't quite control their emotions either.

A long breath of relief escaped from River. Seeing Pancakes unharmed and able to be unzipped from the bag was enough to nearly bring tears to their eyes. But the tears also threatened because that meant it was time for Part Two of River's Reluctant Plan.

This was the part that River *really* didn't like. It was their part, and it was terrifying.

And they had alerted every single monster below that they were there.

On the opposite side of The Monsters' Den, Xavier tied the other end of the rope to a tree after pulling it slack. Clearly he did not have as much faith in his own rope-tying skills, since he then also used both hands to grab it.

He took one hand away for a moment to give River a thumbs-up.

Great. River felt like they might puke.

Their eyes followed the length of the taut rope, now connecting the two forest areas. Unfortunately, they couldn't ignore the pool of monsters below it.

River gulped.

Sure, they had never climbed a rope horizontally—or

in any direction—before. And sure, they didn't do much to improve their upper body strength. And yes, *sure*, one slip and they would be torn apart by too many monsters to count, but . . .

River didn't really know where their thoughts were taking them, but it was not a place they wanted to be. If anything, they felt worse about the situation.

But Pancakes was already on the other side, and so was Avery. What choice did they really have?

With one shaky hand, River grabbed the rope. Xavier had kind of explained how they'd do it, but River figured his knowledge was also limited to action movies and imagination. Plus, he wasn't great at explaining things while unable to show it in practice.

To be fair, River wasn't sure anyone would be able to explain shimmying over a swarm of hungry monsters and really prepare someone else for the experience.

Their other arm was still injured, which wasn't great. Luckily, the injury didn't really affect their fingers. River wrapped them around the rope as well. For a moment, River stared at the rope until the rest of the world went blurry. The rope was the one thing that would keep them alive; it couldn't hurt to focus on it.

Although the rope being the *only* thing keeping them alive was something they'd rather forget.

River switched their grip so that both palms faced inward, and then kicked their legs up over the rope. They let out a breath once they found that they remained hanging and the rope hadn't immediately snapped or fallen to the ground.

Their injured arm hurt and their entire body shook, but they were okay.

So far, so good.

They just had to move.

Holding tight with their legs and one hand, they grabbed the rope farther behind their head. They followed with their second hand and then pulled to slide their legs over. River was glad they weren't wearing shorts anymore.

And they were moving.

Extremely slowly, but moving nonetheless.

Soon enough, the growls increased, both under them and in River's head, and River was completely suspended over The Monsters' Den. There was no more safe ground beneath them. No way to turn back. The noise pounded in their ears.

Still shaking, but keeping their legs locked, they kept moving. There was still something strange about what they were feeling. The usual fear and worry were familiar, but something darker surrounded them. That anger and hunger and yearning for . . . what? River didn't know. It was almost like they were feeling the emotions of someone else.

Or somethings.

They were closer to The Centertrees than ever, and if Xavier was right and The Centertrees were The Otherwoods' source of power, maybe they made the monsters stronger too. Maybe that was why their buzzing echoed in River's head and why the monsters' emotions were messing with River's. Or maybe the longer River stayed in The Otherwoods, the more they became a part of it.

River bit the inside of their lip. They couldn't worry about that now, hanging upside down and clutching the rope.

The one good thing about the position they were in was that they saw only the sky above and didn't have to see the ground below. The bad side of that was hearing the monstrous sounds but not really being able to tell how close they were.

The plan was working, that was what mattered.

River had a chance of pulling it off.

They gained a little confidence in their movements, pulling themself along and scooting down the rope with more speed.

Their palms stung, but it was fine. They were moving. It was fine. The buzz in their head still rose in volume, and River felt like they were underwater with how muffled everything outside the monsters was.

Then something cut through the noise.

Turn back

River's hand slipped and their stomach lurched. Their injured arm shot down, and with their heart loud in their throat, they quickly pulled their arm back up and hugged it around the rope.

It wasn't unusual for a little voice in River's head to tell them how bad an idea was or point out everything wrong with them. It was also known for cataloging every embarrassing thing they'd ever done and throwing it to the front of River's mind at random moments. But this voice was different.

Because the little voice in River's head that had just

spoken didn't belong to River. But it couldn't be the monsters, could it? They didn't speak. At least, not that River knew of.

They could barely hear over the chaos in their head and the pounding of their heart, but Xavier must've noticed that they'd nearly fallen and suddenly stopped halfway. Maybe it was only River's imagination. That made more sense.

River reached their hand out again to keep moving.

TURN BACK

They slipped again, but this time, their injured arm was the one left clutching the rope, and it couldn't hold the weight. That hand fell too, and the world flipped in a rush of color as River's arms fell and only their legs held them on the rope.

They were dangling, midair.

And they could see the monsters.

Snapping their jaws, baring their knifelike teeth, oozing ink and slime and slithering below. Waiting. At the ready.

River's heart pounded so hard, they thought it would explode. They tried to pull themself up, crunching their stomach. It was a difficult move, and they still weren't fully recovered from the last monster's hit. The attempt sent a sharp pain through their abdomen. They were back to dangling, swinging enough that the monsters started to blend in a swirling mess of bloody claws and red-streaked eyes.

They needed to get their grip back on the rope.

Desperate, River swung their upper body, trying to

swing high enough to grab the rope and gain some security. But as they swung their body forward, their legs unlocked.

With the monsters rumbling below them and a distant scream, River fell.

Right into the depths of The Monsters' Den.

25

The Fall

It happened so fast, no one else would've been able to notice.

But in that moment, rushing to the ground and the monsters below, River realized two things:

One, they were probably going to die.

And two, despite all their best efforts and their immense fears, deep down in the very depths of who they were, locked away from the brightest rays of sunlight . . . River truly didn't expect this to end in failure. They believed in themself.

That was an important thing to realize.

And while River didn't know it at the time, it was a realization that was never made too late.

26

The Second Chance

River hit the ground with a thud that knocked the wind out of them. It hurt basically their entire body, but especially their backside, which was weirdly embarrassing even given the circumstances. They saw a flash of light and their skin stung, but they were alive.

They also weren't being devoured by monsters.

Which should've been a good thing but was so unexpected. Given what they had braced themself for, River was wondering why they *weren't* being devoured by monsters.

They opened their eyes, and it took a second for the world to settle back in. The buzz in their head was still apparent, but much quieter, faded into the background.

They could see the rope above their head. That made sense. What didn't make sense was the monsters around them.

All of them were still, watching River. They would have been like grotesque statues if not for the rise and fall of their chests and the occasional blink or ooze.

In their shock, River made eye contact with dozens of them, but they still didn't move. They didn't try to attack.

It was strange and, while certainly preferable to an awful death, a little unsettling. But it felt like a sign. River was able to keep going, and they'd be able to save Avery.

If they finished getting across.

They won't hurt me.

The thought sprang into River's mind around the buzzing, but it wasn't the same as the voice from before. Maybe it was their gut, telling them what seemed like the truth. If the monsters were going to attack, they already would have. This was River's chance.

They had to take it.

Slowly, as if a sudden shift would awake all the beasts from this odd but lifesaving trance, River got to their feet. It hurt, and their palms were rubbed red, but they managed to do it without making a sound louder than their breath.

And the monsters stayed still.

River turned toward the other wall, where Xavier and Pancakes were peeking over the edge. Both seemed to have confused expressions on their faces.

Carefully, River took one step in Xavier's direction.

Only the eyes of each monster, locked right on them,

moved. River held their breath as they took another step, and another, keeping their movements slow and trying to make as little noise as possible.

The last note, written in blood on the tree, crept to the front of their mind: *They are waiting.*

If Xavier was right and the monsters were all connected to The Otherwoods, maybe they were commanded to let River go. Maybe The Otherwoods really did want River to make it to The Centertrees.

For some reason, that thought was scarier than everything else they'd faced. But they had something new mixed in with their usual fear. They had hope. And that felt strong enough to get them across.

Xavier must have noticed River was headed toward the tall cliff, because he took the hoodie that Pancakes had been wrapped in, leaned on the edge so the rock pushed into his armpit, and held the hoodie down as far as it could go.

The sleeve dipped low enough that River would be able to reach it.

They could no longer bring themself to look at the monsters behind them, or focus on the ones in front, all remaining still. At least temporarily, they seemed to be letting River get away.

River grabbed the sleeve. Gripping as tightly as they could, they lifted one leg to find a hold on the rock. It wasn't steady, but the toe of their shoe dug into the side of the wall. Xavier helped them, pulling up on the hoodie until River was able to grasp his outstretched hand. He yanked River up over the edge, and they scrambled to follow with their feet.

Immediately, they collapsed onto the dirt and stared up at the sky. Broken branches still loomed over them, a reminder that soon enough they would be back in the trees.

Still, River took that one moment to be happy they were alive. To have made it that far, even if they couldn't completely explain why. In that one moment, it was enough.

Pancakes padded over to them and licked their face. His scratchy tongue stung a little, so River pushed him away with a smile.

Xavier still looked stunned, his mouth slightly open like he didn't know what to say. Finally, he held out the dirt-and-cat-hair-covered hoodie to River. They put it on, not sure if the chill in the air was the weather or something slightly more sinister.

Finally, Xavier spoke. "Maybe we should find a place to rest."

"Aren't we almost to The Centertrees?" River stomped forward but felt light-headed. Xavier had to steady them to prevent them from falling.

"Yeah, but you're a mess, okay? Let's rest while we can."

They wanted to go after Avery, to make sure she was okay, to finally *save* her, but Xavier did have a point. They weren't a great rescue option at their best, and they wouldn't be much help while barely able to stand.

"Okay," they said.

Xavier stuck out his arm so River could grab it. They didn't want to seem weak, but they also could use a minute to rest. A little recovery nap and some food and they'd be fine. They took Xavier's translucent arm.

"Besides," Xavier said, "we don't know what will be waiting for us at The Centertrees."

River felt a little dizzier, but they'd figured the same thing. And it was terrifying.

But their feet moved forward because failure wasn't an option. And River Rydell, who fought monsters and escaped death, would not fail.

27

The Light in the Darkness

Xavier had them rest in a small clearing not far from The Centertrees. They didn't have much to set up, but River used the opportunity to eat, and gave another tuna packet and water-filled cap to Pancakes. While their near-death experience had taken away some of River's appetite, their feelings weren't far off from those of the happily munching Pancakes.

"Where are The Centertrees from here?" River asked, after finishing a protein bar. They were sitting in a grassier area, which was a little easier on their tailbone than the plain dirt. It still wasn't perfect.

There was nothing that sounded better than a hot

shower and their own bed. Even with Charles underneath. But that would have to wait.

"In that direction." Xavier pointed. "Do you see that bluish, kind of indigo light? It's from The Centertrees."

River's eyes followed the direction of Xavier's finger. Behind the trees they were used to, there was a large ominous glow. River couldn't tell if it came from the trees themselves or the area they were in; too much of it was blocked.

"The Centertrees light up?" River asked. "Like when I touch the other trees here?"

"But way more intense," Xavier answered. "I told you, they're where the source of magic is."

There was something hard and cold in his voice, like he didn't want to talk about it. Which was weird, since getting to The Centertrees had been their goal all along. Maybe Xavier was worried about what awaited them there. River certainly was.

And it wasn't the trees that River was concerned about.

Since Xavier wore a tense expression, River said, "Thanks for helping me. Even if you are only in it for the ice cream, it means a lot. I wouldn't have gotten this far without you."

River probably wouldn't have gotten ten feet past that first monster, let alone all the way through The Cursed Bridge and The Monsters' Den. Although sometimes Xavier said things in a way that really got on River's nerves, he had grown on them.

For a moment, Xavier's expression darkened, but then he smiled. "I'm happy to help. And not just because of the ice cream. *Mostly*, yes, but not only."

River laughed a little. They bent their knees and rested their head on top, moving around a rock in the dirt with their hand. Pancakes lifted his head, eyeing the rock curiously, ready to attack. River tossed it toward him before looking back at Xavier.

"I think you know it's more than the ice cream now, River," Xavier continued. "I mean it when I say you're like a sibling to me."

A bit of warmth filled River's chest. "Me too."

It was a reassuring moment, but it didn't last long. They had Xavier and Pancakes, but Avery was still alone. River didn't know how much time passed since they'd entered The Otherwoods. What horrors had she been dealing with?

"Be honest, will we be able to save Avery?"

Xavier was silent for a long time. It made River's stomach twist, but they did appreciate that he was taking the question seriously.

"I don't know," Xavier said, "but we're certainly going to try, aren't we?"

It wasn't exactly the answer River wanted, but maybe it was what they needed. They never expected any of the journey to be easy, but at least they had someone else on their side.

Someone with opposable thumbs, no offense to Pancakes.

Besides, the fact that they were only slightly disappointed in the answer made River think that they did believe Avery was okay.

And I'll save her.

It was a promise she wouldn't hear but they would keep making until they got her back.

"Let's worry about that after some rest, shall we?" Xavier asked. "You still look horrible."

"Thanks," River muttered.

Since Xavier didn't need sleep, he volunteered to keep watch while River got some rest. Pancakes had already curled back up to sleep, but he would've been a terrible watch cat anyway.

It certainly wasn't their bed, but River was tired enough that even spreading out on the forest floor was comfortable, or if comfortable wasn't exactly the right word, it was at the very least relieving. They stretched out their limbs to loosen their muscles. Their backpack wasn't a great pillow, but it was enough to allow them to fall asleep.

River may have dreamed of Avery, but they didn't remember any of it. They woke with a bad feeling. The world around them was dark, though the sky above was teasing with the first promise of light.

"Sleep okay?" Xavier asked when he noticed River was awake.

River nodded, but they weren't sure it was the truth. Part of them did feel better physically, but there was something off. In the air, in their head . . . they weren't sure. But something wasn't right.

In the woods, a strange purplish light glowed. But it wasn't in the direction of The Centertrees, so it didn't make any sense.

River glanced over at Xavier. "Do you see that?"

"What?" Xavier was looking directly at the light. "I don't see anything."

At first, River thought that Xavier was joking, but his expression seemed entirely serious. River also didn't think it was the time for a joke like that. River had enough experience with this in their own world to know that more likely it was a light that somehow only they could see.

Great.

River knew what they should do, because it was what they always did: ignore it and pretend nothing was there. But what if it was something that had to do with Avery? Would they be able to live with ignoring that?

Xavier would probably go with them if they asked.

Or you can go alone.

River couldn't tell if the thought was their own or the voice from before. But if they'd survived The Monsters' Den because of either voice, they figured they should keep listening to it.

Besides, maybe it would be a test. River couldn't solely rely on Xavier; they had to keep pulling their own weight. If anything, Xavier would be proud of them for facing a potential fear by themself.

Worst-case scenario, they'd scream and run back.

"I have to go to the bathroom," River said quickly. "Number two."

They wanted to get the excuse out before they could change their mind.

"Okay," Xavier said. "Take your backpack and Pancakes

with you in case anything happens. I'll keep watch here, so come straight back after and we'll go."

"Got it."

Taking Pancakes and their things would also bring a little more comfort—like they weren't necessarily walking right into a trap.

River gathered their backpack first, swinging it around to their other arm so it was held by both shoulders. They kept the flashlight and pocketknife out of the bag. They still needed some additional light, and while they hoped they wouldn't need the knife, it was a possibility.

"Remember," Xavier said, "scream if you need me."

River nodded. They picked up Pancakes, who seemed a little annoyed to be woken from his nap, but also pleased that he didn't have to stay behind. He jumped out of River's arms but stayed tight to their side.

"I'll be right back," River said.

Xavier smiled and nodded.

River turned to the strange light. It wasn't far away, but not in clear view of Xavier either. River flicked on their flashlight. Pancakes walked against their left leg, purring.

They could do it. It would be okay.

They took a shaky breath, turning away from Xavier, and walked toward the unfamiliar light.

28

The Return of an
Old Friend

With only a few steps into the trees, River put a barrier between Xavier and them. Following the light carried them a bit deeper in the woods than they would've normally gone. While they weren't far, the branches and tree trunks seemed to give more cover than usual. It was a noticeable difference, and even with Pancakes at their side, River felt alone.

There was something strange about these trees, compared with the rest of the woods. They drooped, sections of bark peeling and dangling off the twisted trunks. The branches didn't reach out toward River as they had before; they were still and cracked. It was almost like this area of The Otherwoods was dying.

But that didn't make sense. They were so close to The Centertrees—essentially the life force of The Otherwoods. Why would the area around it be dying?

River looked away from the sick trees and focused on the light in front of them.

They couldn't tell what it was, other than a bright orb suspended in the air. It didn't seem to be connected to anything. It almost looked like what people would call a spirit in photographs back home, but River had seen plenty of spirits in The Otherwoods, and even the inhuman ones didn't look like *that*.

It wasn't connected to The Centertrees either. To their left, River could see the big glow that supposedly powered The Otherwoods. That was nothing like the bright, condensed purplish light hanging a few feet ahead.

But if it wasn't either of those things, what was it? "Is this a bad idea?" River whispered to Pancakes.

Pancakes looked up, eyes shining in the darkness, catching light from the flashlight. He didn't have any answers, but he hit his butt against River's leg in what they could only assume was a reassuring way.

River approached the light. It flickered and sparkled a little as their viewpoint shifted. Pancakes also looked up at it, eyes wide. He dug his paws into the ground, lifted his butt, and pounced to attack the light.

Although Pancakes gave an impressive jump, it wasn't quite enough to reach the orb.

Maybe he had the right idea in trying to touch it?

River stood directly under the glowing light but still

didn't have a better idea about what it was. They blinked, but it didn't morph into anything easier to understand. Despite how it cut through the draining darkness, it didn't hurt when looked at. If anything, it was inviting. Like it promised something.

Touch it

River froze at the voice in their head. It was the same one that had spoken to them in The Monsters' Den. Maybe it wasn't a good idea to listen to it?

River swallowed.

If what Xavier said about The Otherwoods earlier was right, maybe it was the woods itself somehow communicating with River. And if that was the case, it would make sense to listen. The Otherwoods took Avery for some reason, and River had to do what it wanted to get her back.

With one last look at Pancakes, River squeezed their eyes shut and reached out to the orb.

River hadn't wanted anything bad to happen, but it was a little disappointing that nothing did. They'd expected something—a shock, maybe. A pinch. A slight tingling or burning sensation. But there was nothing.

"Pancakes, did you . . ." River opened their eyes to look at the cat, but he wasn't there. Panic rose back up River's throat, and it took all their effort to swallow a scream and call out his name instead. "Pancakes?"

River looked around, and the panic trickled through all their limbs and shook the tips of their fingers. They weren't in the same area of the forest. They didn't know where they were.

It was warmer, with flames dancing in a fireplace to the right of them. The rest of the room was filled with books and maps and other trinkets that all seemed connected to The Otherwoods. Cautiously, River walked toward the largest map, which was of The Otherwoods itself. The Centertrees was smack-dab in the middle of it, and River could trace the path they took down to The City of Souls.

There were whole sections that were unfamiliar to River, but they didn't feel the desire to look at any of those places. What they had seen was already more than they wanted to.

"Nice of you to finally make it," a voice said.

River turned around, to look right at the face of Natalia, the psychic spirit from The City of Souls. The spirit reclined in a chair, using what appeared to be a small monster feather to paint her nails a blood red.

River's eyes widened at the sight of her. They could think of probably fifty different questions right off the bat, but one particular question pushed its way out their lips first.

"Where's Pancakes?"

Natalia finished the nail she was on and placed the polish and feather on the dark wood side table next to her. She smirked, like she was amused at River's priorities. "He's back with your body, out in the woods."

"My body?" A chill ran up River's spine. "Am I dead?"

Natalia chuckled. "Was I this dramatic when I was alive?" River wanted to point out that she was plenty dramatic in her death, but stayed silent. The psychic blew on her nails.

"You're not dead. I made a mental link, so your mind is here but your body is still there. It's fine, just like taking a nap."

"In the middle of the woods? Where a monster can kill me?"

Sure, the monsters hadn't attacked River at the den, but they didn't like the idea of being so exposed out in the open.

Natalia threw up her hands. "Well, I didn't have much choice! You're the one who continued to ignore all my messages."

River took a breath. It was a lot to process, but the idea of a mental link didn't seem all that far-fetched compared with what they had already dealt with since stepping across the first portal to The Otherwoods. Instead, they focused on Natalia's last sentence.

"Those notes were all from you?" River asked.

"Warnings, more like it. That voice in your head, too. Neat trick, isn't it?" The psychic looked proud of herself.

River's jaw dropped. "That almost got me killed!"

"I don't know why you're upset with me for putting your life in danger," she said, waving away River's concern. "You are plenty good at doing it yourself."

River couldn't argue with that. They were the one who had walked into The Otherwoods in the first place. Sure, they only did it to go after Avery, but it was their fault Avery had been taken in the first place.

They'd broken all their own rules.

"That may be true," River admitted, "but why are you trying to get me to leave? I have to save Avery."

Natalia's eyes narrowed. "How important is your friend to you?"

River swallowed. They thought that was obvious, since they'd come all this way. "She . . . I . . . well . . ." Their face heated.

"Ah, so you *like* her." Natalia chuckled. "I was a lot older before I learned pretty girls would be my downfall."

"You like girls?" River asked. They couldn't help it. They hadn't talked to many queer adults before.

The psychic chuckled again. "I knew I was a lesbian early, just like how you knew you were nonbinary. So it's not that I don't support you liking Avery . . ." As she trailed off, her expression grew grim. She stood over River at her full height. Her bright eyes stared directly into theirs. "But do you like her so much you'd really give up your life, River?"

River's skin itched. They felt small under that stare, and the weight of her words only made them feel smaller. "Why?" River squeaked.

Natalia turned away, shadows playing over her face. "I think it's about time you learn what normally happens to humans who can see spirits and monsters." She turned back with a pained expression. "To other people like you."

29

The People Who Could
See Spirits

River couldn't hear anything aside from their own beating heart, even though the buzz of the monsters wasn't present here. Something in the air shifted a little, like their strange connection to The Otherwoods deepened in a different way. They could hardly believe what Natalia said.

"There have been others?" River asked. "People like me?"

River remembered Xavier mentioning people like them and that he thought it was a myth. No one else had confirmed it before, not even in The Otherwoods.

"Sure, you're special, but not *that* special," Natalia said. "There have always been people like you since people existed. Just not very many. It's a rare thing. I don't know how you lot are chosen, or if it is simply unfortunate circumstances . . . maybe something misaligned in the stars in that one location. I don't know. All I know is what happens after."

River squeezed their hands together. They had kind of assumed they were just extremely unlucky. They hadn't really thought about other people being in the same boat.

"From what I hear, though, they usually aren't called to The Otherwoods quite so young." Natalia frowned. "I guess these are desperate times . . ."

River was a little jealous of those other magic-seers for getting extra time to prepare. It had to be way easier to deal with The Otherwoods as a teenager or an adult. They'd have everything together. River didn't like feeling particularly young, but they also knew they didn't have the experience to prepare for any of what they'd recently faced.

But at the same time, River felt a connection to these people. They didn't know their faces or their names. They didn't know anything other than the idea of their existence, but it still set something afire in their chest.

It was like seeing nonbinary teens and adults on the internet; it made them feel like things might be okay and they weren't so alone.

It was a connection that was more than names and faces. It was a connection that went down deep into what made a person who they were.

"Were you like me?" River asked. "Since you're psychic?"

Natalia shook her head. "No, it's similar, but to a much smaller degree. I was able to feel things, more than the average person, but I never had the kind of power you have. Not even close. That's why I ended up here in The Otherwoods. That little bit of a difference was enough for these trees to capture my spirit, but not nearly enough to be someone like you."

Xavier had been right. A connection to the supernatural was what brought spirits to The Otherwoods. Natalia was like Xavier's brother. With enough of that spark to capture the attention of The Otherwoods.

River, on the other hand, seemed to have the whole fire.

"Did you know anyone like me?" River asked.

Natalia walked over by the fireplace, the dancing flames tossing shadows across her face. It made her seem older, although River didn't know how old she was in the first place. Maybe she had just seen a lot.

"Yeah, I knew a girl," Natalia said softly. "And I loved her."

"A girl?" River asked. "Aren't you like thirty?"

Natalia glared at them. "I died at twenty-five, I'll have you know. But fine. A woman. She was twenty-two, and it was maybe a year or so after I first crossed into The Otherwoods that she arrived."

River thought twenty-five was still pretty old, but they didn't say that, because they knew their mom got really happy when people said she looked thirty.

"What was she like?" River asked. "What was her name?"

They wanted to know everything about the woman. It was the closest they'd ever been to another person in their situation, even if it was only through someone's memories.

"She was like sunshine warming your skin, or cool water on a hot day," Natalia said. "She was always smiling, always seeing the best in everything. Her name was Emma."

Natalia handed a notebook to River. It had a very detailed drawing of the woman. From the pencil sketch, she looked pretty. Like someone everyone would want to get to know.

The psychic watched them absorb the drawing. "You can't take pictures here, and memories fade. I did my best so I'd never forget her face, her name . . . so I can hold on to as much as I have left."

River had noticed that Natalia had used the past tense the whole time. The way she talked matched the emotion in her voice: something like loss. "What happened to her?" River asked.

Natalia looked a little haunted. She quickly snatched back the notebook and closed it. "I couldn't save her." Her eyes were glassy, a few tears spilling down her cheeks. "I couldn't save her, but when you came . . . well, I thought maybe I could save you."

River found it hard to appreciate the thought when they were so freaked out about what it implied. They didn't know what to think, only that Natalia's warnings to get out and turn back felt very appealing.

They found their voice. enough to speak up, even if the words came out soft and shaky. "Save me . . . from what?"

Natalia opened her mouth to answer, but before she could make a sound, darkness poured into the room. The lights hadn't failed, and it was still morning, but moving shadows filtered in from every crack and corner. The same shades as the monsters, they ripped through books and scattered papers.

The two looked in horror as the shadows came right for them.

30

The Biggest of Many
Bad Decisions

The shadowy tendrils covered the walls and sliced through the air. They wrapped around Natalia's wrists and yanked her arms to her sides. One slashed River's leg, causing them to yelp from the sharp sting and producing a thin line of blood. River was frozen in fear as the room filled with more and more of them.

They didn't know what to do.

Finally, they found their footing and raced over to Natalia. River grabbed at the shadows holding on to her arms. They tried to rip them off. But their fingers went through the shadows, and they felt chilled. It was like the spirits seemed to be able to make actual contact when they wanted to. Or maybe River couldn't touch them because they weren't really there.

Either way, there wasn't much they could do to help. River turned, but the entire room was filling with the shadows. They could no longer see the walls, and the shadows crossed over each other on the floor, slithering in like snakes.

"River," Natalia said. "I'm going to break the link."

"What?" River tried to pull at the shadows attacking her again, even though they knew it wouldn't do anything. "What about you?"

"I'll be fine," she promised. "Not much they can do to you here when you're already dead." Her expression grew a bit more serious. "Don't trust anyone, River. You probably can't trust me either, but do one thing." Her eyes burned so intensely, River had no choice but to meet them. "You want to know where the magic comes from in The Otherwoods? Look *inside* The Centertrees."

River didn't get the chance to ask what she meant by that. Just as soon as it happened, the room disappeared, and the world around them faded to black.

Immediately, they awoke to Pancakes' tongue scratching their face. As uncomfortable as it was, River couldn't be annoyed when they were so happy to see him. Although they were still flat on their back against the forest floor, they pulled Pancakes into a hug.

"Sorry for leaving you alone for a little," River said.

The cat purred.

But River disrupted him by scrambling to their feet and fixing their backpack. They weren't sure what was happening, but they had the feeling they needed to get to The

Centertrees as soon as possible. Natalia's words had chilled them, and their gut was saying they had to leave immediately. They were sure Xavier would understand and catch up with them there. If this had something to do with Avery, they couldn't waste any time. River was tired of being too afraid—they had to go after her right then and find out what was really happening in The Otherwoods.

"Are you down to break some more rules?" River asked Pancakes.

Pancakes meowed happily, apparently a rule-breaking kind of cat.

It was against everything that had kept River alive before entering The Otherwoods: ignoring any issues, keeping to themself, letting other people deal with problems, staying quiet even when it came to what they believed in.

It was terrifying. But they had to know.

They could still see the faint bluish glow from the direction of The Centertrees, spreading through the forest.

They had to get to Avery, before whatever had come after Natalia decided to hurt her too.

With Pancakes at their side and their heart pounding in their chest, River ran toward the glow, not looking back.

31

The Centertrees

It was impossible to miss The Centertrees once they got close to them. Both River and Pancakes stopped in their tracks at the sight, Pancakes a few feet ahead. In a clearing in the middle of The Otherwoods forest, a large group of trees had sprouted from the earth. The ones in the front towered, covering the trees behind them, and the air smelled sweet, like honeysuckle and something more. A scent that River couldn't place, but it lured them in and felt like home.

The Centertrees were beautiful.

A kind of beautiful that River hadn't seen before, a kind of beautiful that only seemed possible in dreams. Bright blue light, the source of the bluish glow, stemmed from cracks in the trunks. The cracks were like veins, running the lengths of the trees. It was similar to the glow that the other trees gave at River's touch, but so much brighter. The Centertrees didn't need contact with humans; they already had that incredible light.

Instead of blood, they contained magic.

River could *feel* it.

It warmed their chest, created a buzz that filled the air, and picked up their senses. It was music and moonbeams all rolled up into that hopeful blue. The tops of the trees were an explosion of pastels—flower petals in pinks, purples, oranges. They were so dense that not even the branches could be seen through the floral crowns of the trees.

River was in awe.

And the trees saw River. They beckoned toward them. River couldn't explain it, but they felt the trees calling. Inviting them to come closer. Before they realized it, they were walking toward the trees. With each step, the ground lit up around their feet in that incredible blue, like the color really was in River all along and coming to The Centertrees was returning to where River belonged. While a little more wary, Pancakes followed closely behind.

The field around The Centertrees was barren, a circle of dirt with nothing growing from it. Almost as if nothing else could get close to the trees because they simply couldn't compare.

River had seen plenty of trees in The Otherwoods. Hundreds—thousands, even. But none of them came anything close to the towering trees in front of them. In beauty, in power, in anything.

If River hadn't believed in magic already, they certainly did at the sight of The Centertrees.

Getting closer to them, River tried to focus on what they'd come for. Natalia had told them to look inside The Centertrees. That didn't seem all that difficult a job, given the massive trees' arrangement in something like a circle. Maybe Avery was kept there.

River didn't know what to expect. They were standing right next to the nearest tree and felt so small in comparison. From this short distance, they had to crane their neck back to see the top of it. The ground beneath them was now coated with petals, but apart from that, they didn't sense anything major from the center of the trees.

Hiding behind the trunk, River pulled out their pocket-knife. They'd have to be ready for whatever came after them when they went inside The Centertrees. They didn't have Xavier, but they did have Pancakes, and the cat had recently been much better monster backup than the spirit anyway.

Keeping their footsteps as light as possible, River moved around the trunk to sneak into the middle circle of The Centertrees. Their breath caught as they took in the sight.

There was nothing there. Only the same flower petals covering the dirt.

Now River could easily see all the other Centertrees, lined up neatly in the circle. Otherwise, there was nothing.

Where was Avery? Disappointment and dread washed over River. They'd really believed that Avery would be there. They bit down on their lip to prevent tears from falling.

Had Natalia lied to them? She'd essentially said that no one could be trusted, and that would include herself. But what reason would she have to make up a story like that? Especially when she was the one trying to tell River to go back home.

It didn't make any sense. There had to be something there.

They wondered if they should go back to Xavier for help. Clearly the monsters didn't have Avery at The Centertrees. Maybe they didn't come out at night, which was preferable for many monsters. Xavier would probably know more.

On the other hand, Natalia did want them to see something. Maybe they had only this brief chance before the area was overrun with monsters. It was an opportunity, and something inside them was saying they should take it.

But what did Natalia want them to see?

"Pancakes, what do you think?"

River looked back at the cat, who was hardly paying any attention to them. He was on his hind legs, stretched to his full height and scratching his claws on the tree. They weren't his usual lazy scratches; it was almost like he was trying to dig something out.

Slowly, River approached the tree.

Natalia had said *inside* The Centertrees. Maybe she didn't mean inside the circle they formed but inside the tree itself.

The bark was still beautiful up close, even more so, as River could trace their finger over the blue cracks. The tree was pleasantly warm to the touch. It oddly felt lifelike, like it had a pulse.

River looked up and down the bark. Around eye level, there was a large piece of bark that seemed to be peeling. It almost looked like a chunk of the tree had been hacked off, then returned to close it back up.

They turned toward the nearby trees to see if there was something similar. The one on the right had a large hole. Big enough for River to completely climb inside. It looked like it had been intentionally hollowed out. Maybe the magic had already been emptied? That tree didn't have a strong blue light like the rest of them. It was faded, dying. Maybe that was why a section of the woods didn't look right. Some of the magic was missing.

But how? Why?

River looked back at the tree in front of them. This one was still alive and filled with energy, so they should be able to see the magic underneath. River's heart pounded in their chest, and their hands were shaking with nerves.

What would the magic look like, and why would River need to see it so badly?

With the blade of their knife, they chipped away at the peeling bark, deepening the cuts. Finally, they were able to stick their fingers in the edge and peel back the thickly cut layer of bark.

A human eye stared back at them.

It slowly blinked.

And River screamed.

32

The Girl the Psychic Loved

River had had a lot of bad feelings in their life and spent plenty of time completely afraid. But none of those bad feelings could compare with the bad feeling they had at that moment. And they were sure none of the times they'd been afraid before would compare either. They swallowed the end of their scream and started to peel more bark.

It might be Avery trapped inside the tree, and they had to get her out.

That was their first logical thought.

But logic flew out the window when they pulled away the entire strip of peeled bark, because the sight in front of them couldn't exist with it.

It wasn't Avery. It wasn't anything close to what they'd thought, not exactly.

It was so, so much worse.

There were pieces of a person's face, and what was once a pretty one at that. Two eyes a dulled green, full lips, high cheekbones. But instead of being a rounded head, the face melted into the rest of the tree. Skin mixed with bark, and it was hard to tell where the person ended and the tree began. River could make out a chin and a neck, but then it warped into wood. The blue veins of the tree carried through, connecting to the partial-person and fading into the cracked skin patches with a color like a bruise.

River couldn't see anything below that, and they were thankful for it.

The face they did see—the blend of a tree and a person—was so horrific and gruesome, they weren't sure they could take seeing the rest of the body.

It blinked again, lips opening slightly.

It—she—was alive.

River felt dizzy. Bile rushed up their throat, and before they could stop it, they vomited right into the fallen petals below them. Some of what they heaved up hit the base of the tree, and with wild eyes, River looked back toward the face.

"I'm sorry," they said quickly. "I didn't mean to throw up on . . ." They were going to finish the sentence, but they couldn't get the "you" out. Was the person a part of the tree? Was the person the tree itself? They looked away, both from embarrassment and because it was getting difficult to keep looking.

"Free . . . us . . ."

River glanced around, trying to pinpoint the source of the voice, but unless Pancakes had developed the ability to talk, there was only one horrific explanation. And Pancakes looked as frightened as River felt. His fur stood on end and his ears bent straight back as he looked at the face in the tree with wide eyes.

River followed their cat's gaze back to it. The lips were still parted.

River took in the features of the face, which seemed oddly familiar. While it was questionably human and definitely gruesome, they forced themself to focus on all the features they could make out. To imagine them as a person.

River gasped when they realized the face reminded them of the pencil drawing they had just seen.

"Emma?" they choked out.

The eyes blinked again, and the lips twitched—like they wanted to turn into a smile. It was enough confirmation for River, and once they had made that connection, it was impossible to unsee it.

Emma wasn't dead, not exactly. Instead, she was . . . this.

Which seemed like a worse fate.

"I'll save you," River said. "I'll get you out . . ."

She had said "us." Did that mean every one of The Centertrees had a person on the inside? There were around

217

a dozen, at least, so that meant . . . It was too much. River tried to wave away the thought and the freezing panic that came with it. They had to do something.

They had to cut Emma out somehow. They pointed the tip of the knife toward where it looked like her face ended. River was frozen. How were they supposed to cut her out when she was so morphed to the tree? How bad was the rest of her body? Would she be able to be removed, or did the tree blend with her intestines as much as it did with her skin?

A bit of vomit rose in River's throat, but they swallowed it.

What could they do for her? For any of them? Keep peeling away at the bark? Would that make it worse? River wanted to get Emma out, but she was so infused with the tree, it hardly seemed possible. River didn't want to hurt her.

Emma's eyes looked toward the knife. "Too late . . . ," she breathed out. Her voice was scratchy, earthy. It sounded pained, like she wore it out long ago and hadn't tried to use it again in years. "Must . . . destroy . . ."

Destroy? What? The Centertrees? River wasn't sure how they would be able to do that when they had only their pocketknife on hand. It wasn't like they had an axe lying around the house to bring along on Otherwoodsy adventures.

"I . . ." River trailed off. They didn't know what to say. Words wouldn't come as easily as tears. They couldn't believe this was the woman Natalia had talked about.

There was no light left in her, except the magic swirling

in the bark around her. How long had she been like this? How long did it take to become . . . whatever she was? Questions flew through River's mind, and they felt panicked and scared and a little grossed out.

But one question, one thing they needed to confirm, kept coming back.

After all, this was the closest River had been to someone who was like them. Someone who might have understood them in a way no one else did. And she was tortured, not even quite a human anymore.

"The rest of us?" River asked. "They're in the other trees?"

Emma slowly blinked again, her sunken eyes looking glassy.

River's breath came out too quickly. They were about to hyperventilate. All The Centertrees contained a person. A person like them.

That was the fate of people who could see spirits. The people who had magic. That was what Natalia had been warning them about.

River was dizzy as they looked at the tree toward the right. The one that wasn't shining, the one with the hole carved into it.

Big enough to fit River. To pull on their skin and empty them out and . . . River couldn't finish the thought and keep imagining what it meant. It was too wicked, too terrible.

And it had happened to everyone else. All the people born with their ability, trapped in these hauntingly pretty trees for years.

"No, no, no," River moaned in a whisper. They looked back at Emma. Wasn't there any way to help her? To help the rest of them?

Was there any way for River to save themself?

Pancakes pawed at River's leg, but they could hardly feel him. They opened their mouth to formulate some question for Emma, when leaves started rustling from the other side of the clearing, back in the forest. There were growls and snarls of monsters, still at a distance, but echoing through the air.

Emma forced her eyes over to meet River's, moving her cracked lips to utter one more word.

"Run."

33

The Last Hope

In that moment, River couldn't think about how hopeless the situation was with Emma and whoever else was in the other Centertrees. They couldn't think about how they still had to save Avery and didn't even know where she was. All they could think about was getting away.

River scooped up Pancakes and ran back in the direction they'd come from. They didn't look behind them to see if the monsters had broken through the trees and made it to the clearing. They kept running. Their arms were getting tired from the weight of Pancakes, especially since their injured arm never had a chance to do much healing, but there was no way River would leave Pancakes behind.

They could hardly stomach the idea of not holding on

to the cat. His soft fur was the only thing keeping them going, keeping them from freezing up and crying.

River had to be brave.

They also didn't want to be turned into a tree in an absolutely terrifying way, but unless they stopped it somehow, that seemed to be their fate.

They crossed the clearing and jumped back into the trees. Although they weren't exact about the direction, they darted around trunks and branches to head in the general area of where they'd left Xavier.

He would know what to do. River would explain what had happened, what The Otherwoods was really doing, and Xavier would figure out a new plan. He might have some idea about where exactly the monsters kept Avery, and how they could rescue her and get away safely. There had to be something they could do to avoid becoming like Emma, and if anyone would know the answer, it would be Xavier.

They just had to find him.

River cursed themself for leaving in the first place. They should've gone to Xavier immediately after Natalia had given them the warning. Then they wouldn't have had to face Emma alone, and Xavier would've helped them right away.

What if they didn't find him in time? What if the monsters got to them first?

River kept running, holding on tightly to Pancakes, who didn't squirm. It was like he could sense the utter panic that coursed through River's body. River hardly told their legs to keep moving; they simply did it without asking.

Stepping into The Otherwoods had already been too

much for a person like River. What they'd found in The Centertrees was way past too much. They didn't want to keep imagining the tree cutting into their body, mixing in with their blood and bones. Their vision tunneled at the thought of it again.

Sometimes, River felt like their body didn't quite belong to them. It wasn't the size they wanted, there were parts that they could do without, and plenty of things they would've liked to shift.

But being trapped in a tree, like Emma, would be all the worst of those feelings all the time, alone and in darkness. For . . . River wasn't sure how long anyone would stay alive in a position like that.

They also couldn't imagine anything more terrifying.

Some of their tears dripped into Pancakes' fur, but they had to keep moving. They had to find Xavier, who was really their only hope. River clearly couldn't get through it alone—they were barely holding it together.

They darted around a tree, and something smacked against their leg. Pancakes jumped out of their arms as they tumbled. A few branches scratched River's skin, but more cuts were the least of their worries. As they caught their breath, Pancakes hissed, a few drops of spit coming from behind his sharp teeth.

Heart pounding and eyesight both sharpened from adrenaline and blurred from tears, River turned around.

A monster stood over them, poised to strike. Its shadowy shell was so smooth, light almost reflected off it. It had a long scorpion tail with a sharp barb at the end at least the size of River's hand. Its six arms all had small pincers, which it must have used to grab River's ankles. The face of the beast wasn't much better, with shining blue eyes that opened in vertical slits and a wide mouth.

It hissed back, six forked tongues shooting out in Pancake's direction.

River swallowed.

They knew the monster wouldn't kill them—for whatever reason, the monsters wanted River in The Centertrees—but that didn't mean it wouldn't hurt them. Or Pancakes.

River couldn't let any of those things happen.

They pulled out their pocketknife, holding it tightly in their hand. This monster looked a lot harder than the previous one they'd fought. It was possible the small blade wouldn't be able to pierce it at all. They didn't have anything else to defend themself with.

River tried to scramble to their feet, but the monster lashed out with one of its arms and pinned their left leg in the dirt. They couldn't move it, and more panic rose. Bending like they were doing a sit-up, River stabbed the blade into the arm of the monster.

It didn't break through the exoskeleton.

River's vision clouded with fear. It wasn't enough. They didn't know what to do. They'd be lucky if the monster let Pancakes go. It would take them directly to that tree. River tried to keep breathing as the image of Emma forced itself to the front of their mind.

The monster pinned down their other leg, looming over them with its tail at the ready.

River glanced over to Pancakes, who was staring back with wide eyes. River tried to communicate the message to *run*. Maybe Pancakes could find Xavier and still save Avery, even if River failed.

But Pancakes was a cat, and River wasn't a psychic.

Pancakes hissed and pounced on the monster, trying to gnaw at the arm holding River down. The monster glanced at the cat and changed the direction of its pointed tail.

"No!" River screamed.

Just as the monster twitched in anticipation of the strike, a large form slid underneath its belly, smoothly yanked River's pocketknife out of its arm, and shoved it directly into the neck of the creature. Inky blood erupted from the wound, causing the beast to rear back. It tried to finish the attack with its tail, but the spiked end hit only dirt.

Pancakes jumped to River as the monster fell backward to the ground.

The figure in front of them stood, holding on to the pocketknife and wiping some blood off his leather jacket.

Xavier.

River had never been so happy to see someone else in their entire life. A rush of relief passed through them, bringing out a few more embarrassing tears. Xavier had found them as he promised he would. The spirit had mentioned he was particularly good at finding people, so River shouldn't have worried. Xavier was here and they would figure it out together.

Everything would be okay.

River scrambled to their feet and smacked themself against Xavier, hugging the spirit. He practically went entirely translucent, but River didn't care. Xavier stiffened, and River realized they'd hugged without asking, which was kind of rude. Hopefully, Xavier would understand given the circumstances. They broke away, looking up at him with wide eyes.

All the words poured out at once. After the first came out, the rest tumbled right after it without pause.

"I went to The Centertrees without you, and I'm sorry. I lied about having to poop also, which I'm sorry about as well, but it's bad, Xavier. I saw someone who could see spirits like me and she was literally inside the tree. And not just like trapped in the tree, like she *was* the tree. Her body was all mixed up in it and it was horrible. And I think that's why the monsters are after me. For some reason they want to do the same thing to me."

River wasn't sure they'd given the clearest explanation, but enough of it seemed to get across to Xavier. He wore a sad expression, lips turned down slightly into a frown and eyes looking dead enough to belong on a ghost.

River waited. They knew it was a lot to take in at once, but they were kind of expecting more of a reaction. Sure, Xavier hadn't seen the way Emma looked, so maybe he didn't really understand, but the idea alone seemed pretty messed up, in River's opinion.

A strange moment passed between the two of them, and another bad feeling came over River.

"Xavier?"

The spirit sighed.

"I'm sorry, River," he said. "I didn't want you to find out like this."

34

The Worst Betrayal

River was frozen. Their brain took extra time to comprehend the words. They heard them, but their mind didn't want to accept them, so all they could say was "What?" Xavier didn't answer after that initial pause, and they were able to catch up enough to respond to their own question. "You mean . . . you knew this whole time?"

They wanted it to be a misunderstanding. They desperately wanted that. Or at least, a poor joke from Xavier's sometimes questionable sense of humor. They would say how unfunny it was, but eventually roll their eyes and forgive him, and then Xavier would give the actual reaction they were hoping for.

That didn't happen.

Instead, Xavier only shrugged. "Well, yeah. It's not exactly a secret."

River choked on the air around them. Their eyes burned, but more tears wouldn't come. Instead, they stayed frozen. Their body didn't know how to respond any more than their mind did. They understood the individual words, but they didn't make sense together.

"But . . . why?" River finally asked. "I thought we were friends. I thought we were like . . ." River wanted to say "family" but they couldn't choke out the word. "I . . . You said you would wait for me, I don't understand . . ."

Their voice cracked. They had the same kind of feeling they had when they didn't prepare for a math test and could only stare at the question until their eyes blurred and the letters and numbers were shapes without meaning.

It was like that but, as The Otherwoods tended to make things, so much worse.

Xavier almost looked regretful. "Well, I'll still wait for you, River. I mean, you'll die eventually in there, and then they'll have to hollow out the tree and replace you. When that happens, I'm guessing your spirit will be able to pass on."

There were times when River really appreciated how positive Xavier could make things sound, but this was certainly not one of those times. He spoke like he honestly didn't see anything wrong with what he was saying. River's chest hurt more.

Not only had Xavier known about it, he didn't really want to help River at all. He spoke like River's fate was already sealed, like the only option was to face the same curse as those before them.

"You *guess*? You don't even know? You promised you'd wait for me, and you don't know if my spirit will be able to pass on?" River asked. They weren't quite sure why they asked that. They had a bunch of questions, most of them worded in a much meaner way, but that was the one their brain settled on.

Xavier shrugged. "I've only been here two years. It takes a lot longer than that for them to need a replacement." His expression lightened. "But I wouldn't worry about it, I'm sure you'll appear totally human again once they do have to replace you. I don't look the way I did when I died. I know dying in The Otherwoods isn't ideal, but I mean, a death is a death, right?"

His happy tone made the words somehow worse. River didn't know how to explain that an untold number of years in that situation—lonely and torturous—with only a body that wasn't quite theirs and thoughts that were too slow to fade hardly seemed the same as any other death. Not even close. River wanted to scream. River wanted to punch him in the face. River wanted to be angry.

But River was still River, so they found their tears again instead.

"But . . . why?" they choked out.

Finally, the slight smile dropped from Xavier's face. He looked guilty, but maybe River was reading into it. They couldn't be sure Xavier cared about them at all at that point. It certainly felt like he didn't. Maybe it didn't matter anyway.

Xavier clearly didn't want to help River, so they figured they'd be better off alone.

They didn't wait any longer for an answer, even though they asked the question in the first place. River turned on their heels to run.

Something pulled on River's wrists, stopping them in their tracks. They fell to the dirt, arms extended. River turned back to see one of the shadow tendrils that had attacked Natalia.

Xavier frowned. "It's a little late for running now."

The shadows crept around Pancakes, also stopping the cat from running. The two of them were stuck.

"How are you doing this?" River asked Xavier.

The spirit shook his head. "Those aren't me. That's all The Otherwoods. It's a little desperate at this point."

River tried to pull away from the shadows, but it was hopeless. They were frustrated, and fresh tears spilled from their eyes.

"Look, River," Xavier continued. "It's nothing against you. Really. I like you, a lot. You're a great kid. I wish there was another way, but there isn't."

Xavier took a step toward River. River crawled backward, but the shadow tendrils didn't let them go far. Besides, Xavier still had the pocketknife. They didn't have any way to defend themself, and they were trapped. Pancakes was trying to bite the shadows, to no avail. He was annoyed, but it wasn't like the cat could understand the weight of the conversation.

River should've listened to Pancakes earlier. He'd never seemed to like the spirit much.

But it was too late for should-haves.

"Another way for what?" River asked, the anger finally coming forward. "I don't understand. Why? *Why?* Why is this happening? Why does it have to be this way?"

They thought they at least deserved a clear answer. Xavier sighed, as if it could possibly be a pain to give them one. Pancakes pawed in the dirt toward River, possibly sensing their distress, but the shadows kept them apart.

Xavier finally spoke. "The Otherwoods is powered by magic, but it can't produce any itself. Magic used to be believed in, even when it wasn't accepted. They prosecuted people like us. Killed us, banned us from The Elsewhere. But The Otherwoods gave us a home after death, River. So in return, we gave it our magic."

River's mind raced. They couldn't believe Xavier had known this all along. "But . . . what's different about me? About . . ." River wanted to say "The Centertrees," but it felt weird to refer to them as a thing when there were people inside.

"Back in the land of the living, people started to believe in magic less and less as the years went on. Because of that, those with magic never truly embraced their power—they hid it and let it fade away. That led to fewer people being born with it, and more importantly, fewer people dying with it. Without as many magical spirits passing through the afterlife, The Otherwoods was running low on power. It needed to go directly to the source. There was no choice but to lure in those living with high amounts of magic. People

like you are essentially live batteries for The Otherwoods."
Xavier bit his lip. "It all sounds a little gruesome, sure, but
you don't get mad at a cat for killing a mouse." Xavier gestured to Pancakes, his gray body completely covered in the
shadow tendrils, only his head, tail, and claws exposed. "It's
doing what it has to do to keep living."

River gulped. They couldn't find the words to explain
how, but they felt the situation was very different. At least
cats didn't lie to mice for days, pretending to be their friend
and treating them like a sibling. Cats didn't torture mice
for *years* before putting them out of their misery.

And maybe it was wrong of River, but they felt that killing them, River, wasn't quite the same as killing a mouse.

"So whenever one person dies now, The Otherwoods
finds another to replace it?" River could barely get the words
out. That was all they had been to Xavier, to The Otherwoods, the entire time. A battery.

"Exactly," Xavier said. "But there's been a little too much
time since one of you was born. The situation got much worse,
River. That's why The Otherwoods has been calling you
from when you were young. And it certainly took you long
enough to get here! We're in a bit of a tricky situation. It
has to be you, River. And now. Otherwise, this whole place
will die."

River squeezed their bound hands into fists. Natalia
had said it. Normally The Otherwoods would wait before
luring them in, but it was desperate. It had needed River
the entire time, which was why it had called to them as
early as River could remember.

Ignoring the calls was the only thing that had kept River alive. Then River had given The Otherwoods an idea—to use someone they cared about against them.

And River had fallen right into the trap.

They looked at Xavier, even though it was hard to see his face. It was the same spirit, but it felt like River was seeing him through a carnival mirror. It was distorted, not right. What he was saying and doing didn't match who he was.

Except the truth was, River hadn't known the real Xavier at all.

"But why did you work so hard to get me here? Why do you care if The Otherwoods dies or not?" River asked.

There wasn't an answer that would make any of it okay, but River still had to know.

"If The Otherwoods dies, I'll have to pass on. I told you, I can't do that without my brother." His voice lowered a little. "Honestly, I'm not sure I want to at all. The other spirits, they don't care. Half of them want to pass on, as if they know what's next—as if they know it's *better*. Can you imagine? That kind of risk?" Xavier shook his head. "They don't understand. They choose not to. But I see The Otherwoods for what it is. Something powerful. Something that actually cares about people like me, my brother, all of us, when no one else has. But we can get revenge. Overtake those other realms and show them how strong our magic is. Those in *The Elsewhere*"—Xavier spit out the name like it hurt to say—"and even those back home."

River gaped. "You can't be serious. You want to bring all these monsters to the real world?"

"To the *living* world," Xavier corrected. "I hate to break it to you, but this is all very real. Of course, that won't be until after we destroy The Elsewhere."

"That's not fair," River said.

For the first time, Xavier really looked angry. His eyes flashed as he twisted to River. "Not fair? What's not fair is dying as a teenager. What's not fair is realizing that you don't get a normal afterlife because you weren't allowed into the right spirit realm. That's not fair, River." Xavier took a deep breath, composing himself. "But we—I—can make it right."

"But . . ." River didn't know how to end the sentence. No word felt quite strong enough. "Why you?"

Maybe it wasn't the right wording. Was it like Natalia said and Xavier had some small psychic ability that attracted his spirit to The Otherwoods?

"Why *you*?" Xavier countered. "I said I'd do anything to protect The Otherwoods, to stay here. The Otherwoods saw that in me, while the other spirits were content to fade away. It knows I'm helping it and that I'm willing to do what needs to be done. I'm not afraid."

River didn't know what to say. They *were* afraid. Afraid and helpless and heartbroken. They could only look at Xavier in horror, but he pasted back on his brightest smile.

"Come on, stop being so dramatic. You think I wanted any of this at first? No. But sometimes things happen that you don't want. So you'll suffer a little. I'll be waiting for you here after it all. I can visit you at The Centertrees from time to time. With my brother, too. We can all be a family! Who knows, if he has a long life, you two will probably be spirits at the same time."

River swallowed. They already had a family. They looked over at Pancakes, who stared back at them, waiting to escape from the shadows. On top of that, they had Avery, who accepted them as a friend and always stood up for them. They had their mom and dad back home. A mom and dad who, even when they didn't understand them, loved River regardless.

They had so many reasons to get Avery and go home.

They had to get out of there.

River's head filled with the loud buzzing once more. New emotions washed over them, not just fear and panic, but that unfamiliar, inhuman hunger.

Skin crawling, River turned to see the monsters. Dozens of them, blocking every direction. There was no way they could get past that many monsters, and they probably couldn't outrun them if they did.

River was trapped.

"Look," Xavier said, voice meant to sound kind. "I understand that you're scared. It's okay to be. I mean, who wouldn't be scared in this situation? But you don't really have a choice here, River. The Otherwoods has Avery and now Pancakes, too. It played nice all this time, but it will hurt them to get what they want. It sucks, kid, but you're out of options."

River's stomach sank lower and lower. They were almost surprised it didn't drop right out of them. But Xavier was right about that much. The monsters had Avery. Even if they managed to escape the shadows gripping their wrists and get Pancakes back, River couldn't let Avery die.

Even if they did want to, their chance of success was right next to zero.

But the whole reason they'd stepped into The Otherwoods was to save Avery. It was River's fault that she was there in the first place. She didn't deserve any of it.

River glanced over to Pancakes, who stared back with his bright eyes. He blinked slowly, as if saying he'd agree to whatever River wanted. Pancakes meant the world to River, and had fought for them the entire time. River couldn't let anything happen to him either.

River didn't know how to save themself, and they were starting to think they couldn't.

But maybe they could save those they cared about.

River's voice was soft, but they knew Xavier could hear them. "If I go through with it, will Avery and Pancakes be set free? Unharmed?"

Xavier smiled, like River was finally starting to understand something. "Of course. If The Otherwoods has what it wants, there's really no reason to touch them or keep them here."

"I need you to promise me," River said. "You'll let them get out, back to the world of the living, and make sure neither of them gets hurt."

Xavier gave a small smile. "Well, I suppose it's the least I can do." He held out his pinkie. "Promise."

River eyed the blade that was held tight in Xavier's other hand. "How can I trust you?"

"You can't," Xavier said. "But I don't have any reason to lie now. And you don't have any leverage. So here we are."

There was enough humanity in Xavier's eyes that River could maybe believe him. With River in a Centertree, Xavier would get his way. It wouldn't benefit him to hurt Avery or Pancakes. And the spirit seemed to care very much about what benefited him.

Slowly, River connected their own pinkie, watching as the spirit's finger nearly disappeared.

They didn't have to say anything else. A promise was a promise.

"Sorry you won't get your ice cream," River said, their tone a little bitter.

Xavier only laughed. "I guess we all have to make some compromises, huh?" His expression fell a little, maybe from the weight of what he would do next, River wasn't sure. The spirit let out a long breath. "Well, it's about time to head back and say our goodbyes, huh?"

He started in the direction of The Centertrees.

The monsters closed in, and River and Pancakes had no choice but to follow.

35

The Bittersweet Reunion

River felt like a prisoner, but the walk back to The Center-trees was like some sort of twisted parade. Monsters lined the entire way and filled the clearing surrounding The Centertrees. River wouldn't have been surprised if every monster in The Otherwoods, aside from the ones stuck in The Monsters' Den, showed up like it was a popular live event. They seemed to be on the same page as Xavier in keeping The Otherwoods safe.

River didn't exactly want to feel bad for the monsters—they had plenty of reasons to feel worse for themself—but they weren't sure what would happen to the monsters if The Otherwoods died. Would they move on like the spirits, or would they die along with it?

They certainly couldn't bring themself to want any of this on behalf of the monsters, and it didn't make them feel better about the situation in the slightest, but it was a thought that crossed their mind.

The Centertrees loomed in front of them. The walk across the clearing felt shorter than before. River was afraid, but it was almost like they hadn't quite accepted what was about to happen to them. Like they still had to hold on to the hope that they would be able to get out of it okay.

But it seemed that the feeling was deep, *deep* within them. Because at surface level, and maybe a few levels under that, the situation felt entirely hopeless. The Otherwoods knew that—the shadows were gone from River's wrists and Pancakes' body. They couldn't run, not when the monsters had Avery.

Pancakes brushed up against River's leg as they walked, and it was heartbreaking that he had no idea what was going on. River only hoped Pancakes would forgive them at the end of it all.

They approached The Centertrees, and standing right in the center of them was Avery. River didn't think anything would have brought them relief at that moment, but the sight of her still managed to cut through everything else and do so.

She was alive. She looked unharmed. She was okay.

River tried to take in all the details to see how she was. Her clothes were dirtied, but not torn like she'd been attacked. She didn't look particularly hungry or thirsty, so

Xavier may have been telling the truth about the monsters keeping her safe and alive to lure River.

He had known all along, probably.

It was a small relief, despite everything. Sure, Avery's arms were tied behind her back, and she had to be incredibly confused and scared, but she would get out of it. She would survive.

Avery's face lit up at the sight of them. "River!"

River couldn't help themself. They rushed up to Avery and untied her arms. The monsters and Xavier didn't seem to care—it was probably already enough for them that River had come. Once she was free, River faced Avery.

"Are you okay?" River asked.

"I've been better." Avery sniffled but then smiled. "I'm okay, though."

River was just so happy to see her. They'd done it. They'd found her.

And she was going to be okay.

That's what mattered.

River met Avery's brown eyes. "Can I hug you?"

Avery laughed a little despite herself and nodded. River pulled her into a hug.

"Thanks for coming after me," she said.

"Well, I sort of got myself captured."

"Valiant effort, though."

"I promise you'll get home safe, okay?" Pancakes approached them, curiously sniffing Avery before rubbing his head against her leg. "Pancakes too," River added. "You remember my cat?"

"I wish it wasn't here, but I'm so happy to meet you, Mr. Fluffy Pancakes," Avery told the cat, scratching his head. Her eyebrows lifted as she looked back at River. "But what about you?"

River didn't answer the question. They glanced over to the monster next to them. It was the same one that had taken Avery in the first place.

"I'm surprised he let you untie me," Avery said.

River took a moment to speak. "You can see the monsters now?"

"Apparently a side effect of being dragged into their world." Avery shrugged. "Which is useful, I guess. But not sure how helpful it is, considering we're outnumbered."

River didn't want to think about how many monsters surrounded them. River thought that Avery was handling the entire situation shockingly well, but when they looked at her hands, they noticed them shaking.

They had to get her out of this, no matter what.

"It seems that way, yes," River said. "But I promise you're going to be okay."

Avery blinked. "You keep leaving yourself out of those statements."

River stood up, willing themself not to cry. Not then, in front of Avery. "Thanks for always being so nice to me. You're the coolest person ever, and I'm glad I got to know you."

Avery's expression grew more concerned. "What are you going to do, River?" She almost looked angry. "Please tell me you aren't trying something ridiculous on your own. Let me help you. If we get out of this, we do it together."

River's heart sped a little, finally for a reason other than fear. Avery standing up for them was sweet, and if anyone could almost make them believe in not giving up, it was her. Her tone of voice was so matter-of-fact and kind, it could make anyone believe in the impossible.

But River had enough heartbreak that day. They couldn't put Avery in danger too.

"Then neither of us will get out," River said. "I promised myself I'd save you."

"Did you ever think I might want to save you, too? Maybe think about what I want?" Avery asked.

River shook their head. "Sorry, I'm going to be selfish on this one." They wiped at their face, which had heated out of embarrassment. "Can you take care of Pancakes for me? At least get him home?"

"River, stop talking like that," Avery said.

River couldn't look at her anymore. It only made them feel worse. Instead, they turned their attention to Pancakes. They scratched behind his ears. His tail was puffy; he must have been nervous from all the monsters surrounding them.

"You're the best cat ever, Mr. Fluffy Pancakes." River looked right into the gray tabby's eyes. "Thanks for always being there for me. Even here. I love you."

Pancakes slowly blinked. River wanted to believe that he understood how they felt, in some ways, but River knew he couldn't.

River turned around to where Xavier waited with a few monsters by the large tree with the hole. The tree that would light up brilliantly once it tore into them and slowly seeped away the magic they supposedly created.

They glanced around at the monsters surrounding The Centertrees. There were so many of them. It really did seem hopeless. But only for River.

River turned back toward Avery, Pancakes at her side, and forced a little smile.

"I'm doing something I never thought I'd be able to do," River said. "I'm being the hero."

Despite the fear that filled their body, the hero turned around and started walking toward their fate.

36

The Unexpected Hero

Xavier put a hand on River's shoulder. It now made River's skin crawl, but Xavier tried to put kindness in his voice like he couldn't tell. "You're making the right choice, River."

It seemed like an awful thing to say when they didn't have much of one.

River stared at the tree in front of them. It looked dark inside the hole, but they knew the darkness was the least of their problems.

It was hard to tear their eyes away from their gruesome new home. But through the cacophony of monster sounds, a more familiar buzz grew.

River snapped their head in the direction of the sound—Charles. River blinked, but the giant bug-like creature didn't disappear. He didn't look like the illusion on the bridge either. It was regular old Charles. River almost laughed despite the weird betrayal that stung them. After all the less than pleasant times the two had spent together, Charles was happily waiting for River to lose their humanity and die.

He was certainly acting strange about it. Almost a little too into the idea of River's demise, in their opinion. Instead of standing around at the ready like the rest of the monsters, he was rubbing his bladed arms gently up and down the Centertree that would soon entomb River.

It didn't really do much, except leave his oozing slime all over the bark.

It looked like Charles was oozing more than usual. River could follow his trail—it looked like he'd gone all the way around The Centertrees, rubbing himself over each one.

What a weird monster.

"You know each other?" Xavier asked, looking between River and Charles.

"Sort of," River answered. "He's the monster under my bed. Or was, I guess."

Xavier nodded as if that was a perfectly reasonable and normal answer. "Ah, the famous Charles! Oh, well, that's very cute you'll be the one to save him, then. All of us."

River knew that wasn't true. Preventing a spirit from passing on could hardly qualify as saving them. If anything, whatever waited for Xavier on the other side would likely be a lot better than The Otherwoods. The bar was low.

River knew who they were saving, and they were both

currently yelling at them to stop. Well, Avery was yelling. Pancakes was meowing. But the same sentiment was there.

Xavier was still eyeing Charles as he oozed all over the place. "Weird. Maybe the lights aren't all on upstairs."

River was a little offended on Charles's behalf. He might have been terrifying, but he was almost like family. River could call their bedroom monster weird, but no one else could. Charles had plenty of lights on; he was the one that told River to bring Pancakes along with them.

River glanced back at Charles. River had thought it was a mistake, that Charles hadn't meant to help them, but . . . what if he had? Xavier held on to River a little tighter. "Ready?"

River gave one last glance to Avery and Pancakes. They had no idea if the two of them would really get out safely. They couldn't imagine what Avery would say if or when she did get back. How could she explain what happened to River to authorities?

To River's parents?

River's eyes burned again at the thought of their parents. They couldn't count on either one believing Avery. Maybe River would be able to tell them when they were all spirits. Their vision blurred, and they wished they could see their mom and dad one more time.

But The Otherwoods wouldn't give them that. It wouldn't give them anything, and River would just have to accept it.

"Okay," River said, "I'm ready."

"Really?" Xavier asked.

"No," River said. "But I'm doing it anyway."

It almost could have been a nice exchange that called back the adventure they went through together. If Xavier hadn't wanted River to die a horrific death the entire time. That was certainly enough to put a damper on any relationship.

But the familiar words came out loud and clear. River didn't think anyone would be ready to become one of The Centertrees in such a gruesome way, but something in their gut told them everything would be okay.

They didn't feel ready, they felt brave.

Xavier pulled the backpack off River, and the items inside scattered as the bag fell on the ground. No one made a move to pick them up. River supposed their things didn't matter much given what they were about to do.

River approached the giant tree. They reach their hand out first, to place it softly against the bark, trying to avoid Charles's slime. The tree immediately responded to their touch. It trembled, sensing the magic inside River. The bark around River's hand gave a dull blue glow.

The tree needed more. It was hungry. Branches reached out and twisted River around, gripping them tight.

As they were pushed into the tree, time slowed. They didn't fall into the hole all at once. Their back and hips were pulled in first, the bark having slid across their skin to latch on to them. They still had time to see Pancakes, biting the monster that guarded Avery so the two could run toward River.

Xavier took steps forward to face the oncoming duo. Charles buzzed. River looked over at him once again. Perhaps the monster thought he too deserved a goodbye. Instead of waiting for a farewell, Charles used a bladed limb to slide an object to the base of the tree.

It was the lighter that had fallen from River's bag.

The Centertree continued to latch on to them, a piece of the tree tearing through River's shoulder blade. River mashed their teeth together in pain but looked down.

Right at the lighter, still within reach, and the slime sparkling on the base of the tree.

They realized a few things in that moment.

One, merging with the Centertree would be a horribly painful experience that they certainly did not want for themself, or anyone else in the future.

Two, Charles was further from a monster than most humans (or once-were-humans).

And three, despite everything, they *were* a hero. And no matter how much the odds were stacked against them, heroes never gave up.

River yanked away from the Centertree's grasp, feeling bark and skin rip from their shoulder, and picked up the lighter from the ground, flicking it on. They twisted their body to toss the open flame at the tree and jumped out of the way.

The fire caught on Charles's very flammable slime, and immediately blazed up the side of the Centertree.

Within seconds, the entire tree was engulfed in flames.

37

The Dancing Flames

As much as River could hardly believe their own actions, they didn't have time to stand around and stare at the flames covering the tree that they were supposed to be inside. They couldn't focus on the pain of their shoulder, or the fear they still felt.

They had to move.

Charles buzzed to get River's attention. He leaned down, and River understood to climb onto the back of the monster. Once on top, River held on to Charles's neck, and the monster ran. They could hear Xavier's scream, even through the chaos of crackling fire and wood and the now feral, uncontrollable sounds of the monsters. River thought it was toward them, but it could have just as easily been for

Charles. "Are you kidding me?" Xavier yelled, strained voice carrying after them. River could hear him try to collect himself with a cough. "River! Come back here, *now*."

Charles's trail was effective: the flames quickly spread from tree to tree, moving around the entire circle. River looked back to see Emma's tree start to burn.

They felt terrible, but they thought back to her words. How The Centertrees had to be destroyed. How this way, they wouldn't be able to hurt anyone else who was born like River or Emma.

They really hoped it would be over quickly and she would be free like she wanted.

"We'll fix this," Xavier called, seemingly speaking to The Otherwoods itself. "I'll fix this."

Was that still a possibility? River knew they had to get as far away as possible. The heat from the fire warmed their back. The back of their shirt stuck to them with blood, and the front was stained with some of Charles's ooze.

Charles ran up to Avery, who held Pancakes in her arms. River reached down a hand to her, and she grasped it. They pulled her and Pancakes up. Sitting on the back of Charles, Avery held Pancakes tightly with one hand and clung to River with the other. River's heartbeat picked up, but now wasn't the time.

Behind them, Xavier and a herd of other monsters raced after them.

Charles was faster than expected and managed to break through the circle of The Centertrees before the flames coated them all. A wall of monsters still faced them. They were all different shapes and sizes, some looking animalistic and some not looking like anything River had seen before. Charles didn't slow. Instead, he raised a bladed arm and sliced through one of the other monsters. Monster blood splashed onto River's and Avery's faces, and they tried not to gag. Charles kept going, racing across the clearing and into The Otherwoods forest.

"Don't get me wrong, I'm glad we're running away, but why were they trying to shove you into a tree?" Avery asked.

They brushed past the first layer of trees. The tired branches drooped down toward River, like even the trees wanted to reach them for a bit of magic.

"To steal my magic?" River knew that wasn't a great explanation, but they didn't have time to completely catch up Avery. "Sorry if I get blood on you; the tree tried to cut me open so it could morph with my body."

"*What?!*" Sometimes you didn't need to see someone's expression to guess what their face looked like. Clearly, their explanation wasn't great.

River swatted away branches that were getting particularly close. Charles did a good job of weaving around the trees, but River, Avery, and Pancakes jostled on his back, struggling to keep from sliding off onto the dirt.

"Yeah . . . I was told if I went through with it, you and Pancakes would get to go home safely. But I'm glad Charles was there to help me. I like being all human, actually."

It took a moment for Avery to respond. "That's . . . wild." Pancakes, tucked between the two of them, meowed in agreement. "You'll have to explain more when we're not running for our lives. I'm assuming this is Charles? I didn't expect you to befriend a monster."

A branch slapped River's face, stinging the skin. They winced and lowered themself closer to Charles. "We have a history. He's been living under my bed for months."

"Oh," Avery sounded like it was too much to bother denying, so she simply went along with it. "I never thought I'd say this after the past few days I've had, but I am so glad to have this monster in my life. You're amazing, Charles."

Charles, although a bit preoccupied with fleeing for all their lives, buzzed happily.

Even though his exoskeleton was a little slimy and hairy and gross, River hugged him tighter. They didn't know what they would have done if the monster hadn't showed up. But they couldn't go off on a heartwarming monologue then, because they could still hear the rapid footsteps behind them, sounding closer and closer.

With The Centertrees burning, River figured there was no reason to keep any of them alive anymore.

"How do we get out of here?" Avery asked.

It was a very good question. One that River wasn't quite sure they knew the answer to. They looked around them, but there was nothing among the trees. Only the same gray and blue-tinted trunks, racing by them as Charles ran forward. Some of the bark seemed to crack in places that didn't look natural.

Was it because The Centertrees were burning? That was good, but it wouldn't be if they didn't find a way out soon.

"A portal. We need a portal," River said. "But usually The Otherwoods itself opened up those to lure me in, and I don't think it's very happy with me now."

"Great," Avery said. "So we're winging it."

"You're taking that well."

"It's worked for me in English class all year."

"This might be a *little* different."

Charles slowed down. River was about to say something, but they looked ahead and saw they were nearly at The Monsters' Den. There would be no way for them to get across without getting torn apart by the monsters below.

River was pretty sure those monsters wouldn't go easy on them now.

Charles quickly made a turn to the left, but a few monsters caught up to them. He snapped to the right so quickly, Avery had to tighten her grasp, making Pancakes yowl, but a handful of monsters came in that direction too. They were cornered, and even Charles couldn't break through. Through the buzz of emotions in River's head, they felt a separate, cutting frustration.

River tried to give Charles a reassuring squeeze as he stopped.

From behind, more monsters slowly approached, along with Xavier.

He smiled. "I'm almost impressed, River. Burning down The Centertrees? I never would've guessed you had it in you. And you." He turned to Charles. "All that time in the living world severed the link, huh? You aren't connected to the hive mind anymore."

Charles made a noise that was something like a satisfied growl.

That explained why Charles wasn't listening to The Otherwoods like the rest of the monsters. But why was River still sensing his emotions separately?

The monster shook a little under them, and River gave him a pat. Maybe it was similar to Natalia's psychic link. Charles was able to separate from the hive mind but was still drawn to River's magic.

It was almost a sweet thought, if not for the hard face of the spirit staring right at them.

"Really got me on that one," Xavier said. "Totally unexpected." His eyes rolled over to River. "But, River. You can't really expect me to let you all go, can you? If The Otherwoods is going down"—the spirit pulled out the pocketknife blade and pointed at each of them individually—"you're all going down with it."

38

The Most Wonderful
Monster

River knew they didn't have any weapons, but they slid off Charles's back anyway. Keeping in front of their friends, River stepped toward the angry spirit.

"It's over," River said, keeping their head high. "The Centertrees are burning, and they can't take magic from anyone else. Your world is dying."

Despite the distance, they could see the thick, dark gray smoke filling the air. River could feel the difference too. The magic that once buzzed around The Otherwoods was fading, and the effects were already visible. Around them, the cracked tree branches started to shrivel, curling into themselves or breaking to dust and ash.

Xavier followed their line of sight to see his world crumbling around him.

"It could've been so good," he said sadly. "I really would've waited for you."

"I know." And River really did believe him. Maybe after decades stuck in that tree, River would've been able to forgive Xavier, be a part of the family he'd imagined for them. But they couldn't have done that to themself, to countless other people who would've been born with the wrong stars in the sky, or whatever gave them the cursed ability. They couldn't do that to Avery and Pancakes and their parents. River had spent too long avoiding caring about anyone, avoiding getting other people wrapped up in their confusing and often scary life.

But River realized their friends and family weren't stuck with them and the monsters that followed. They made the choice to be a part of River's life, spirits or no spirits. Avery chose to be their friend. Their parents chose to love them for exactly who they are, even when they didn't totally understand it. Pancakes had chosen to protect River again and again. Even Charles chose to betray his own kind to be there for River. There was too much for River to live for. "But it isn't worth it, Xavier."

Xavier shook his head. He looked back at the monsters. And they closed in.

In a flash, Charles scooped River back with his limb and tucked them under his body along with Avery and Pancakes. Charles's body jerked as the monsters reached them, clawing and biting at him. The bug-beast groaned with each attack.

"Charles, no!" River said, pushing against Charles's body to try to get out from under him. They weren't sure what they would do if they did get out, but they couldn't let Charles die for them.

Still, Charles wouldn't move.

"What do we do?" Avery asked.

River didn't have an answer. They were far outnumbered and had no real way of fighting back. They closed their eyes, trying to think of anything.

They were desperate.

They needed something.

Someone please help, River begged whatever was listening.

And strangely enough, someone was.

Perfect timing, the voice in their head said. Natalia's voice. **I just got away from those pesky shadows.**

Hope flooded through River as the sounds of beasts falling echoed around Charles. River was able to push around Charles's arms to regain sight of the battlefield. Now the group of them were separated from Xavier and the monsters by the psychic, holding a large sword she had used to slay the monsters that were attacking Charles. It dripped with their red and black blood.

"Of course," Xavier said to her. "It was you that corrupted River."

"The only corrupted one here is you," she snapped. "I thought you were trying to *help* River."

"I am," Xavier said simply. "I was helping them do what they were born to do."

With the monsters' attacks stopped for the moment, Charles lifted himself off them. River ran next to Natalia.

"How do we find a portal?" they asked, voice low.

They didn't have much time.

Natalia kept her weapon at the ready but darted her eyes to River for a moment. "It's magic that opens those portals, and last time I checked, the only thing left with magic here is you." She gave a quick smile. "Sorry I was late to the bonfire. I came as fast as I could."

It was more than enough she was there then. There was still a problem, though.

"How am I supposed to open a portal?"

"I don't know, kid. You're the magic one. Listen to your instincts or something."

"That's not helpful."

"I just offed like five monsters for you, you ungrateful—"

Her words were cut off by more monsters charging toward them. Natalia's eyes widened before she looked back at River. "Go to Charles, figure it out." Natalia glanced back at Avery. "Hey, other kid. Can you fight?"

Avery shook her head. "My teachers say I'm a fast learner?"

"Good enough." Natalia pulled a long knife from her waistband and tossed it toward Avery. She caught it in her hand, and River thought that was one of the coolest things they'd ever seen.

"I definitely don't know how to use weapons," Avery admitted.

"Stab and hope for the best!" Natalia yelled as the first of the monsters reached her.

With no other option, Avery held up the knife in front of her and ran to join Natalia against the onslaught of monsters. River wanted to help them fight, but they knew the best way to help would be to get them all out of there, so they ran to Charles and Pancakes.

How could they open a portal home? It's not like they had anyone to show them the way.

They tried to push hard to summon some kind of magic, but it just made them fart out of nerves. River quickly looked up in embarrassment, but Natalia and Avery were too busy slaying monsters to notice or hear.

But they had to do their part.

They looked at Charles in desperation. "How do I use magic?" River asked. "I don't know how. I didn't know I had any magic in me."

They weren't really expecting an answer. Charles took a bit of a beating, and Avery was only able to tie some strips of clothing around the worst of his wounds. But the creature blinked slowly, clicked his pincers a few times, and then reached out to gently touch the tip of his bladed limb to River's chest.

It left the goopy slime on their shirt, but they understood the sentiment.

Natalia and Charles were right. They'd made it through The Otherwoods, they'd made it back to Avery. Even when they were so scared they almost felt like crying, they'd kept going forward. They'd listened to their gut and they'd made it that far. They would be able to make the portal.

And it wasn't just their ability, whether or not it was a curse. It was who they were as a person. Someone who would do anything for their friends. Someone who could.

They were brave. They were unstoppable.

And yeah, they were magic.

Closing their eyes, River focused on the feeling of the magic inside them. It rose too easily, almost like it had been waiting for River to really look for it the whole time. They let it swell, dance within them.

And they thought about home.

About their mom and dad. About Avery's mom and the smell of her cooking. About the kiss of summer heat, the flowers beginning to bloom. About ice cream, the smell of baking cookies, and curling up with a good book on their comforter.

They thought about all the things that made them happy to be who they were, and desperate to go back to where they belonged.

A sudden rush of heat washed over them.

River opened their eyes, and there it was. A massive portal, bursting with energy and light. It had all the smells and sounds of home. It was their way out of The Other-woods, to put this nightmare behind them.

"I did it!" River shouted. "I actually did it!"

Natalia had her sword lodged deep in the throat of a monster, and Avery was on the back of a monster, choking it with her arms. Both of them gave bright smiles as the monsters they attacked fell to the ground.

They started running toward River and the portal.

River turned back toward it, only to slam right into Xavier's chest.

The spirit's eyes were hard and black as he looked down at River.

"Pretty impressive portal," he said. "Looks like you have an unusual amount of magic in you." Xavier held up the pocket-knife to River's face. "Maybe if I let it out, it will be enough to start over."

39

The Ones Who Were Lost

River's heart was in their throat, and they wondered if that would somehow make it easier for Xavier to kill them. It didn't seem right, but it was hard to think clearly when an angry spirit who was supposed to be your friend held you at knifepoint.

Out of the corner of their eye, they saw Natalia and Avery run toward them. Avery used her knife to wipe some of Charles's slime off her, then slid the knife across the dirt. It landed right at River's foot.

They couldn't get any farther, because monsters rushed in to hold Avery and Natalia back. They looped tentacles and closed claws around their arms so neither of them could get away.

"I'm sorry, Xavier," River choked out.

They tried to reach the blade, but the knife was too far to get without shifting position. And if they moved to pick it up, Xavier would cut their neck open.

"It's a little late for that," Xavier said.

River felt a cat against the back of their legs. Then cold metal pressed against their hand. Pancakes must have picked up the knife in his mouth and lifted it so River could grab it. They didn't think. They gripped the handle and plunged the knife directly into Xavier's stomach.

Out of shock, the spirit dropped the pocketknife, and it left a small, shallow cut on River's cheek before clattering to the ground. Despite the pain, River felt relieved.

Until the spirit gave them a look.

"Did you forget I'm already dead?" he asked.

River looked down at the knife, which had gone through Xavier's translucent body.

Right. That was a bummer.

Pancakes ran off with the pocketknife toward the trapped Avery, Natalia, and Charles. Even though monsters had grips on them, they were at least near the portal. If anything happened to River, they still had a chance of escaping.

Xavier pushed River into the dirt, holding their arm down with one hand so he could take the knife. River pushed back and try to hold on to it, but Xavier was bigger and stronger. He took the knife and loomed over them.

"It won't be so bad, River," he said. "We'll still pass on together, won't we?"

River could hear Avery scream as Xavier lifted the knife over his head. River could only stare at the tip of the blade that would soon be in their chest.

They couldn't move. They could only brace for impact.

But then Xavier was thrown off them, and a delicate hand reached out instead. River blinked as they grabbed it, and were greeted by the face of Emma. She was her whole self, no longer mixed with the tree but a once-human spirit that shone.

She smiled, and it felt like sunlight. "You did enough, River. Let us take it from here."

As River got to their feet, they looked at the other spirits, one for each Centertree that had burned down. They were holding back the monsters. One of them, a man who looked a little younger than Natalia, grabbed Xavier and held his arms behind his back. He struggled, but the adult spirit overpowered him.

Tears pricked River's eyes as they looked at the faces of the spirits. The ones who were lost when they were put in The Centertrees.

It was like Emma could read their thoughts.

"The ones who you freed." She put a hand on River's shoulder. "Thank you."

All of them, though now spirits, were just like them. People who had seen monsters their whole lives, people who had been lured into The Otherwoods and didn't have anyone to believe them. Although they were all older, River could feel the magic in them all. It was familiar, and overtook the chaos of the monsters still in their head. The connection between River and the monsters seemed to get smaller and smaller, like there was no room for it now that the freed spirits were reclaiming the power they'd lost. The monsters around Natalia and Avery let go. Their red eyes seemed confused.

Was The Otherwoods getting too weak to control the monsters?

River looked back at the spirits, but they forgot the question at the sight of the smiles. River looked at each spirit and saw a reflection of themself. In that look, River could sense it.

They were all free. And they wouldn't be trapped again.

"Emma!"

Both of them turned to see Natalia sprinting in their direction. River wouldn't have thought it was possible, but Emma seemed to light up even more. The two spirits pulled each other into a hug and kissed.

River kind of felt like they were interrupting a moment.

"I'm so sorry," Natalia said. "I tried to help you."

Emma brushed it off, holding on to the psychic like she'd never let go of her again. "You helped River, and that's more than enough." She looked over at River and winked. "I think you ought to be getting home."

River swallowed. "What will happen to the spirits that can't pass on? Where will they go?"

"You don't have to worry about that," Emma said. "Without The Otherwoods, they'll be able to make it to The Elsewhere. Where we should've gone all along."

"I don't know, love." Natalia cupped Emma's cheek and smiled. "I'm ready to pass on now." Her loving expression shifted to a playful glare as she turned to River. "Would you just go home before you join us as spirits?"

Behind them, The Otherwoods continued to crumble. It wasn't clear how much time they had left.

"Yeah, thanks. For everything."

The psychic almost looked embarrassed. "'Bye, River." It was more forceful than emotional.

River gave a final wave to the couple, then ran to join Avery, Pancakes, and Charles. They all moved toward the portal, but River couldn't help but look back at Xavier.

He stopped struggling, his eyes meeting theirs.

The spirit had told River that The Otherwoods chose him because he wasn't afraid. River knew it was the opposite. Xavier was just as afraid as River was. Of nothing. Of everything.

But he had let his fear consume him, and the hole it emptied inside him allowed The Otherwoods to jump in.

River could see it then in those light brown eyes that had once held warmth.

"You're not nothing, Xavier," River called. "And you'll never be gone, not completely."

It almost looked like the spirit smiled, but maybe it was a trick of the light. Maybe, just maybe, it was that little bit of humanity still left in him. The glowing shard that would wait for Other River, and maybe even River too, wherever it went next.

River had to believe that there was a trace of the boy

they'd looked up to in the spirit. That maybe it wasn't all a lie. But they wouldn't find out any time soon. There were more pressing matters at hand.

With the trees breaking apart around them, they looked back toward Avery.

"Ready?" she asked.

"Absolutely," River said. And they meant it.

The once-human, freed spirits waved at the four heroes as they crossed through the portal together.

40

The Way Home

Before River opened their eyes, they knew they were back. It was the way the air felt, the sounds of birds and the cars passing on the nearby street. Yet nothing could compare with the relief they felt when they opened their eyes.

They were in Avery's backyard, at the edge of the woods, exactly where she was first taken. River looked around. Avery was next to them, smiling brightly. Pancakes was peeing at the base of a tree.

But . . . Charles?

It should have been impossible to miss a giant bug-monster.

"We're back!" Avery exclaimed. "We did it!" She pulled River in for a hug. "Not to sound like I have no faith in you, but I totally thought we were going to die like ninety percent of the time . . ." At River's tense body, she pulled away. "What's wrong?"

"I don't see Charles."

The two of them looked around frantically. For better or worse, the monster had saved their lives. They wouldn't be home at all without him.

"I don't think I'd be able to see him now," Avery said. "But I wanted to thank him at least."

River glanced around, wondering if they'd somehow missed him in the darkness. They moved across the ground, and stepped in some slime. A trail of it, leading back in the direction of River's house.

They laughed, hard and loud, all the tension spilling from them.

"What is it?" Avery asked.

"He just left," River said. "He left a trail behind."

"Where did he go?"

"He went home." River pointed in the direction of Avery's house. "And we should probably do the same."

River scooped up Pancakes, and the three of them headed across the backyard. They looked terrible, with dirtied clothes (or dirty fur, in Pancakes' case) and cuts and bruises, but they were alive, and they were together.

The things that really mattered.

Through the sliding glass door of Avery's house, they could see Avery's mom, sitting at the table with River's parents. They all looked worried, but everything was about to be all right.

Avery smiled at River and held out her hand.

With the hand that wasn't holding Pancakes, River took it.

Fingers intertwined, the two of them knocked on the glass.

41

The Ending

"Are you ready to go, River?" Avery asked as she adjusted her backpack on her shoulders. The last bell had rung, and they were both meeting River's dad outside for a ride home. They'd been hanging out a lot more after school since everything became relatively normal again.

Well, as normal as it could be with their parents making good on their swear to never let River and Avery out of their sight ever, ever, *ever* again.

When they miraculously reappeared in Avery's backyard, the grown-ups stuck with their original theory: that Avery had gotten lost in the woods, and River had gone back out after her, Pancakes by their side. Didn't matter that the two of them were covered in monster blood when they showed up again or that River's injuries went far beyond what a run-in with a tree branch could do. But sometimes you just can't change people's minds. One thing remained the same from the real story to the fake one, though: River was a hero.

Not that that had made things any better at school. Sure, it was way better now that Avery was officially River's friend, but again: sometimes you just can't change people's minds.

That didn't mean River couldn't change other things, though.

River shouldered their own backpack. "Yeah, just have to make one stop first."

The two of them walked down the hall in the direction of their history classroom. River saw a semi-human spirit drifting past the lockers. It had the face of a human but something like antlers sprouting from its head and a second face on its neck. It looked right at River.

Although River could still see monsters and spirits, no more portals to The Otherwoods had opened. But even without magic, there were still cracks for otherworldly creatures to slip through.

River smiled and winked at the spirit. The spirit's second face grinned back.

Avery and River stopped in front of Ms. Deery's room, but River walked in alone.

Ms. Deery's blond bun was pulled back tightly, and her mouth was a thin line as she looked up at River.

"What do you need, River?" she asked.

Except she didn't. She used the other name.

"It's River, actually," they said, back straight. "And the

fact that you refuse to use my real name despite constant reminders is something I mentioned to the principal this morning." River didn't look away as Ms. Deery's eyes grew uncomfortable. They only looked away to grab an extra copy of their new class schedule from their backpack.

River stepped forward and placed it on Ms. Deery's desk.

"I just wanted to let you know personally that I'm transferring from your class to Ms. Howard's class." River smiled as the teacher glanced down at the paper. "Ms. Howard also agreed to help me start a Queer Student Alliance here. I look forward to seeing you at our fundraisers, ma'am."

It was a challenge, and Ms. Deery couldn't step up to it. After all, River had slayed actual monsters. Monsters like Ms. Deery weren't scary anymore. Not when their power revolved on how afraid they were themselves.

River closed their backpack. "Well, that's it. So, maybe I'll see you next year." They turned around, then looked back with a smile they couldn't hide. "Then again, maybe not."

With that, River turned out of that classroom for the last time.

After slaying that monster and now back at River's house, River and Avery were side by side on River's bed, holding their Nintendo Switches. Having found out they shared a love of Pokémon, they spent a lot of time playing together.

Really, they spent a lot of time together in general.

As friends.

Avery leaned her head on River's shoulder, curly hair tickling their face.

Well, just as friends for now anyway.

Pancakes rested between their legs, wanting to have the barest amount of contact with both of them while still touching them. Despite being River's cat, he had taken an immediate liking to Avery. In a short time, they had gone through a lot together. Certainly enough to develop a kind of bond.

A knock sounded on the half-opened door. River's dad stepped into the room, all smiles. He held up a plate. "I brought cookies. Don't tell your mom I'm letting you eat in your room."

"We won't make a mess," River said. "I promise."

Their dad winked and set the plate on the bed. He eyed Avery's head on River with a smirk. "You know, I think we need to have a talk soon, River. When I was a little older than you, I—"

"That's great, Dad!" River interrupted, face heating. "Let's talk later. We're kind of in the middle of the game."

"Okay, okay." He held up his hands in defeat. "But puberty is nothing to be embarrassed—"

"*Thanks, Dad.*"

Chuckling, he walked back out of the room. River immediately snatched a cookie to cover some of their embarrassment. Avery took her own.

"He's nice," she said.

"Please don't," River said. "Let's pretend that didn't happen."

She smiled. The two were perfectly normal kids, with a

perfectly normal cat. Nothing out of the ordinary, and beautifully regular.

A large bladed arm gripped the side of the mattress, slowly moving in the direction of the cookies.

River rolled their eyes. "I can see you, Charles. Just come out and get one."

"Hi, Charles!" Avery called, trying to look in his general direction.

Charles pulled himself out from under the bed and took two of the warm cookies, buzzing happily as he stuffed them between his pincers.

Just two perfectly normal kids, who were friends with the monster under the bed.

River and Avery laughed, trying to save some cookies for themselves as Charles pleaded for more with his puppy-dog eyes (or the creepy bug monster version of them, which was almost as effective). Pancakes stepped off the edge of the bed to avoid the cookie crumbs, jumping onto the window ledge, then settled into a comfortable loaf shape.

Inside the house, everything was warm and perfect. Through the laughter and chatting, they didn't notice the scratching on the window behind Pancakes from an eerie branch, bent like broken bones. It stretched up from the dirt, looking completely different from the trimmed green grass around it, and reached toward the window.

Scritch . . . scritch . . .

The branch bent toward River's bedroom, and just beneath the cracked gray surface was the smallest glow of a brilliant blue.

Acknowledgments

The journey into The Otherwoods has been both an exciting and a scary one for me, and I simply couldn't have done it alone. I am so grateful to everyone involved in helping me craft this story; each of you helped me get back in the headspace of a kid again, hiding under the covers with a book and a flashlight and seeing monsters in the shadows.

First, I have to thank Thomy, my husband and best friend, for naming the feline icon that is Mr. Fluffy Pancakes. But also for being so supportive and helping me every step of the way. I wouldn't be able to do any of this without you. I love you, from this realm to the next.

To my agent, Jordan Hamessley, for putting up with me when I first pitched this book (and the idea of me writing middle grade in general) after I was already twenty thousand words into the story. I can't thank you enough for believing in my writing and providing guidance along the way.

To the incredible team at Bloomsbury. First, of course, to Alex Borbolla, whose genius editing really took this book to the next level. I'm so glad we were able to continue to work together on this project (and hopefully will for many more). You are amazing! Also eternally grateful to Kei Nakatsuka, assistant editor; Diane Aronson, senior production editor; and my marketing and publicity team: Lily Yengle, Ariana Abad, and Erica Barmash. This is truly a dream team of incredible talent and insight that would impress even the cleverest of creatures (like Charles)! I am so lucky to have you all work on this book.

A special thanks to assistant art director Jeanette Levy and cover artist Kristina Kister for creating a cover that is so incredibly cool, spooky, fun, and perfect. It is a dream come true to see River, Pancakes, and the terrifying Otherwoods so brilliantly brought to life.

Everyone knows a trip to The Otherwoods without a cat companion is asking for trouble, which is why I have to include my amazing writer cats, Jasper and Twinklepop. You both are my Pancakes and just as paw-sitively purr-fect. Even when you're walking across my keyboard or in front of the computer as I'm trying to write.

To those who dared to enter The Otherwoods before anyone else: Alex Brown, Sydney Langford, Elle Gonzalez Rose, Leanne Yong, Sandra Proudman, Shannon A. Thompson, Anca Demeter, Zach Humphrey, and SJ Whitby. You all gave such invaluable feedback, and your brilliance and friendship make me a better writer and a happier person.

My amazing QS group, always: Kate Fussner, Caroline Huntoon, Ronnie Riley, and Jen St. Jude. Seriously, what would I do without our chats? (Cry.) You are all incredible writers and incredible friends.

To my MG groups: both the MG 23 Debuts, which holds so much talent and some of the best books you'll ever read, and the MGty Ducks, who took a YA writer like me under their wing (pun intended) to be my first community of middle grade writers. A shout-out to L. G. Robbins, who is a truly epic writer and reader—I can't thank you enough for all your support!

To my family that supports me, especially my mom, who has been reading my work since I was barely older than River. I think we always knew I'd be an author someday, but it would have been a lot harder without you.

A huge, huge, monster-size thank-you to all the book-sellers, librarians, teachers, book influencers, and reviewers who have supported my work so far and made me such a happy and grateful author. I can't possibly list you all, but the bookish community is truly incredible and the work you all do is amazing. Thank you, thank you, thank you!

Most importantly, to the reader. From one booklover to another: I hope you had fun reading about River's journey, and maybe even saw a little bit of yourself in them. Things are scary out there, but don't let that stop you from being your true self and holding on to that magic inside you. To the trans and nonbinary readers, you are my heroes and my inspiration to cross even the hardest obstacles and cursed bridges. This book is truly for you.

All in all, thank you for entering The Otherwoods. I know firsthand how dangerous a place it can be and I'm so glad you made it out alive.

But maybe keep an eye out for any strange portals—those glimmers in the air, tree branches bent in a way that isn't quite right . . .

Just in case.